CW01646438

THE THIRD LAW

An Abaddon Books™ Publication
www.abaddonbooks.com
abaddon@rebellion.co.uk

Published in 2014 by Abaddon Books™,
Rebellion Intellectual Property Limited,
Riverside House, Osney Mead,
Oxford, OX2 0ES, UK.

10 9 8 7 6 5 4 3 2

Creative Director and CEO: Jason Kingsley
Chief Technical Officer: Chris Kingsley
Head of Books and Comics Publishing: Ben Smith
Editors: David Thomas Moore,
Michael Rowley and Kate Coe
Marketing and PR: Remy Njambi
Design: Sam Gretton, Oz Osborne and Maz Smith
Cover: Michael Carroll & Pye Parr

Copyright © 2014 Rebellion 2000 AD Ltd.
All rights reserved.

Rico Dredd created by
Pat Mills and Mick McMahon.

ISBN: 978-1-78108-098-6

No part of this publication may be reproduced, stored in a retrieval system, or transmitted in any form or by any means, electronic, mechanical, photocopying, recording or otherwise, without the prior permission of the publishers.

This is a work of fiction. All the characters and events portrayed in this book are fictional, and any resemblance to real people or incidents is purely coincidental.

RICO DREDD THE TITAN YEARS

THE THIRD LAW

MICHAEL CARROLL

ABADDON BOOKS

WWW.ABADDONBOOKS.COM

Mega-City One
2079 AD

Prologue

It was an accident, of course.

Yes, I was extorting that citizen. And, yes, that was a crime. I admit that. I've never denied it. I knew what I was doing, and I knew it was technically wrong. Especially for a Judge.

But what so many people have failed to understand is that there are *degrees* of wrongness. Killing a man without due cause is clearly wrong. Accidentally killing a man when you only intend to wound him is marginally wrong, but mostly just unfortunate.

My brother Joe didn't see it that way. To him, the world is divided into two groups: lawbreakers, and Joe Dredd.

I tried to explain, of course, but Joe wouldn't listen. All he saw was me drawing my Lawgiver on Virgil Livingstone. Without context, it looked like I was gunning down an unarmed citizen. But Livingstone wasn't a citizen, not really. He'd given up that right the moment he chose to be a lawbreaker.

And breaking the Law *is* a choice, no matter what any smug liberal do-gooders might tell you about "poor upbringing" and "broken homes." That stomm doesn't sit well with me. Never has.

Some perps will argue, "Hey, I didn't *know* that was against the Law!" but that's not a valid excuse. Just as it's our duty as Judges to make and enforce the Law, it's the citizens' duty to learn and understand it. The basic rule of life in Mega-City One is this: if you wouldn't do it when a Judge was watching you, then *don't do it*. That shouldn't be a difficult concept to grasp, but apparently it is.

A few days after we graduated, Judge Wagner was approached by a perp who wanted him to arrest her friend because he'd sold her a dud batch of crawbies. Wagner asked her, "You understand that crawbies are illegal, citizen?" and the woman said, "Yeah, real ones are, but these ones are *fake*. So are you going to arrest him or what?"

I've seen it myself, too. During my final assessment as a rookie, Judge Kenner and I were on foot-patrol when an ordinary car pulled into a taxi-only bay right beside us. The driver jumped out, saw us, realised what he'd done, looked back at his car for a moment, then turned to us and said, "It's all right—I *am* a taxi-driver. I'm undercover."

So sometimes the people need a reminder of who's in charge. They need to be shown that the Judges are there to protect them from themselves, as well as from each other. In the average week in Mega-City One, four citizens die as a result of possessing a strong sense of curiosity, a fork and a power outlet.

I believe that, in general, people are reasonably smart. But by Grud the dumb ones are *so* dumb they drag the whole damn human race down. This is why you'll always find finger-marks on a wall next to the *Wet Paint* sign. It's why the hinges on car doors are at the front: so that if the idiot driver chooses to open the door while hurtling along the freeway, the wind won't rip the door off and take her arm with it. It's why the food safety laws insist that banana skins and coconut shells must be printed with a warning notice that reads *Don't Eat This Part*.

My first week on the job I stopped a citizen from attempting to pry open the elevator doors on the fiftieth floor of the No-tell Motel. Poor drokker didn't understand the concept of elevator shafts: he thought that there was an endless stream of elevator cars, one after the other, like train carriages, and all he had to do was open the doors and step in.

That's why the citizens need Judges.

I graduated the Academy of Law with the highest cumulative score ever recorded. Joe was a little behind me. Not much, but it was clear which of us was the better Judge. In fact, that had been obvious pretty much from the start.

October 2073, six years away from graduation, Judge-Tutor Semple called our class to assembly. Semple was a stern man. Never smiled, never gave praise, but by Grud we sure knew it when he was disappointed. There were thirty-one of us, then, down from forty the previous year. Semple lined us up and strode back and forth along the line, scowling down at us in silence.

That's all he did. Striding back and forth, glaring with his good eye, saying nothing. And then, maybe ten minutes in, Cadet Milo Lange sagged, turned around, and walked away.

Semple seemed pleased with that. He said, "Hope the rest of you learned something here. Dismissed."

Cadet Gibson wouldn't let it go. He said, "Sir? What did Lange do?"

"Hell if *I* know," Semple said. "Did *something*. Guilty conscience. He'll be gone by morning."

Later, back in the mess hall, Gibson said, "That wasn't right. Lange's a good cadet. He's never done anything wrong."

Joe said, "He must have; he cracked. Semple didn't accuse anyone of anything, didn't give Lange the evil eye any more than he did the rest of us. It was a fishing expedition, that's all. He played the odds, figured that there was at least *one* of us has done something we shouldn't have."

"It's sick," I said, and Gibson and Hunt agreed with me.

Joe sat back in his chair and scratched at the fuzz on his chin. "No, it was a good move. Weed out the weak. I reckon we can expect a lot more stuff like that in the next few years. We're down to thirty now, started with over a hundred. By the time we hit the streets in '79 there'll be maybe ten of us left."

Before I go on, I should make something clear that many people don't seem to realise. The Academy of Law graduates a lot more Judges than that every year, of course. I mean, ten extra Judges hitting the streets each year isn't going to make a lick of difference in a city of eight hundred million citizens, is it? There are multiple classes taking place all the time: our class was one of forty-six. As the numbers whittled down they'd sometimes merge two classes, but mostly the tutors tended to keep the classes separate. The *actual* number of graduating Judges in 2079 was around five hundred, I think.

Anyway: Gibson said, "You and Rico'll be safe, whatever

happens. The two of you could piss on the Chief Judge's boots and he'd give you a free pass." Then he grinned. "Maybe that's what they want, huh? Hound the rest of us out so that the only Judges on the streets will be Fargo's sprogs. An army of interchangeable clone Judges stomping around without minds of their own."

And then he added, "No offence."

I didn't care—Gibson was always saying things like that, trying to get a rise out of Joe. My brother didn't respond, but I could tell he wanted to. Even then, Joe was a Lawbook on legs. He knew the regs inside and out, and never once broke a rule. I knew the regs as well as he did, of course, but I understood the difference between blindly following the rules and understanding their intent.

Judges don't just dispense the Law, we *make* the Law. That's why we have to be the best of the best. That's why, I guess, Semple and the other tutors were right to have been so hard on us.

Long before I graduated, I came to understand the need for Judges to be flexible. If we see two creeps beating the stomm out of each other on the street, protocol says we arrest both and sort it out later. So that's the arresting Judge, a crew on a pick-up wagon—three Judges at least—to take them to the closest Sector House, another couple of Judges there to process the arrest. And then we find out that the creeps are brothers or something like that, and neither will press charges. Best we can do is fine them for disturbing the peace. Fifty creds each, if it's their first offence. That's anywhere upwards of six Judges involved, all for a measly hundred credits.

But say the Judge on the scene breaks up the fight and instead of arresting them on the spot he demands to know why they're fighting. He figures out it's just a scuffle, no harm done. He gives them a warning—not anything official, just a scare—and sends them on their way. Now instead of five or more other Judges having their time wasted, we've got two scared citizens who'll be keeping their heads down for a long time afterwards.

That's why my arrest numbers weren't as high as Joe's. That's why the citizens on my regular patrol routes grew to respect me, not fear me. I'd pass them on foot or on the bike and they'd nod a greeting. A couple of months on the job and I had most of the local juve gangs in line. Half of Joe's were in the cubes.

Sure, the juves would get a bit wild from time to time—they were kids, it's to be expected—but I'd wade in with the daystick and crack a few skulls. Let them know who's boss.

I guess that's where the split between me and Joe really started.

At the investigation, it was suggested an incident in the Cursed Earth when I was a cadet exposed me to radiation that, somehow, affected me. I'd broken my arm and fractured my skull. This was thrown into the mix as a possible explanation for why I "turned bad."

But I didn't turn bad. Not then, not ever. "Bad" and "good" are not absolutes. They're points of view.

Even if I hadn't fully recovered, that theory doesn't make a lick of sense, no matter how thin you slice it. Joe was with me the whole time, only a few metres away. He was exposed to the same levels of radiation that I was. Anything that affected me would have had the same effect on him. After all, we're physically identical.

There were other theories raised at the investigation... My DNA was tainted. I'd been exposed to the wrong sort of propaganda. My constant top-of-the-class scores had gone to my head, made me believe that I could do no wrong, and—therefore—I'd developed the notion that anything I did was right.

But the truth is a lot simpler that any of that. Joe concerned himself with maintaining the status quo, a case of "If it ain't broke, don't fix it." But I could see that it *was* broken. I saw the flaws in the Justice system, and I was smart enough to know how to make everything better.

One

THERE WAS THIS juve, Evan Quasarano. Seventeen years old, built like a tank and almost as smart. Quasarano was a rising star in a gang called the Beadles. They didn't get up to anything too serious; at worst, they did a little flash-mobbing every couple of months, swarm through a store and pick the shelves clean.

Some Judges follow the regs and will do whatever it takes to break up the gangs, but right from the start I knew that was the wrong call. Leave the gangs intact and let them police each other, but keep an eye on them—that's the best approach. If they do become a problem, it's a lot easier to corral a thirty-member gang than thirty individuals each with their own agendas, bolt-holes and alibis.

Quasarano was inducted into the Beadles when he was fourteen. At that age, he was already close to two metres tall, though he was skinny then. A couple of the older kids started giving him a hard time—part of his initiation, I guess. Quasarano took a few punches, hit the ground, then got back up and really laid into the drokkers, just using his bare fists. One of them ended up in the infirmary with cracked ribs and a dislocated shoulder.

They admired that, and soon Quasarano became their foremost enforcer. He kept the younger kids in line, and he was the one they sent out to "negotiate" with the other gangs in territorial disputes.

Like most of the juve gangs, once the kids reached eighteen they were nudged out, whether they wanted to leave or not. Around the time I came on the scene, Quasarano was fifth in line, and the four guys ahead of him were long past their eighteenth birthdays, but they didn't want to go. I can understand that, from their point of view: they'd spent years building up their little power-base and there was no way they'd be happy to just hand it down to someone else.

Quasarano didn't do anything, but he made it clear to the others that they weren't welcome any more. He began to ignoring the older kids' instructions, started telling the younger kids how things would be run. The older guys didn't like that, so one night they ambushed him coming out of a shuggy hall. Four against one.

I got the call and arrived to see Quasarano pushing himself off the ground, covered in blood. The other four looked like they'd tried to take down a tank by running at it with their faces.

"We were jumped," Quasarano said. "This buncha guys... They came outta nowhere and..." He stopped when he realised it was me. "Aw, man. Rico, look... I was defending myself."

I climbed down off my Lawmaster and strode over to him, hauled him to his feet. "I warned you about fighting on my patch, Quasarano."

"Rico, come *on*, man." He painted a bloody streak across the back of his hand with his mouth. "You know me. You know these guys. And you know the situation. They're too old for the club."

I planted my hand on Quasarano's jaw. "Hold still and shut up." I turned his head left and right. "Doesn't look like your nose is broken."

I stepped back and looked around at the other gang members. Three of them were unconscious; the fourth, a nasty little scuzzball called Paxton, was faking it. Compared to the others, there was barely a scratch on him. I'd seen that before, with street-fights; someone quickly realises that he's out of his depth, so he hugs the dirt in the hope he'll be able to slither away when it's all over.

Quasarano said, "Rico, I—"

"You weren't here. Go home. Now."

He hesitated for a second, then took off.

I pulled out my radio. "Control, this is Dredd. Four to pick up, my location. Brawling, four years in the cubes."

From the ground, Paxton said, "Four *years*? No way!" He rolled onto his side, pushed himself up.

I put away the radio. "Then it's a good thing for you that I didn't *actually* call it in. This is how it's going to be around here, boy. You and your friends stay away from Quasarano and the rest of the gang. Understood? Your time is over. You're done."

Paxton slunk over toward me. "Look, Judge... That guy doesn't know stomm from stew. There's no written rule about how old someone hasta be to be in the club. And it *is* a club, not a gang. We're not—"

He shut up, then, because a fist in the face will do that.

I reached down, grabbed his arm and hauled him to his feet again. "I asked you if you understood, Paxton. All I want is a *yes* or a *no*."

He squinted at me through bloodshot eyes. "I'm just sayin'..."

It took two more punches and a solid kick to the ribs before Paxton came around to my way of thinking.

The next day, I saw Paxton and his friends on the street. Not one of them gave me any sass. They kept their heads down as they passed me by. That's part of what it means to be a Judge. We don't just rule the people, we *guide* them. It's better to steer the citizens away from trouble instead of just waiting for them to break the Law and then punishing them.

Joe could never see that. A week after the incident with Quasarano and Paxton, Joe and I had some downtime, a half-hour between shifts where we both happened to be in the same Sector House at the same time. We were only four months out of the Academy, and already we had better arrest records than Judges twice our age.

I spotted Joe in the mess hall. He was always easy to recognise, even from behind, because he was the only one sitting alone. The only one paging through the Lawbooks as he ate.

Joe turned around to face me before I was even halfway across the room. To anyone else, that might suggest some sort of mysterious link between twins or something, but I knew Joe better than that. If he *had* to sit with his back to the door, he'd arrange it so that he could see a reflection in the window, or in the side of a napkin dispenser. I'm not saying he was paranoid, just cautious. There weren't many people who could sneak up on Joseph Dredd.

Joe nodded to me, then to the chair opposite. I put my tray down, and for a moment I watched him eat. Even when we were kids, he was an efficient eater. Food was fuel to him, that's all. I don't ever recall him having a favourite flavour, or doing something like eating the pseudopeas first to get them out of the way. He just ate. Methodically, without any interest other than topping up the body's fuel and nutrients. He shovelled it in, chewed, swallowed, and stopped when the plate was empty, or when he was full. Those two things usually coincided, because Joe never put more food on his plate than he thought he'd be able to eat.

"Hey, Little Joe... Anything interesting today?"

"The usual. You?"

"Not much. Took down those three perps who've been tapping on the Galleria escalators. You'd have liked that—one of them had a zip-gun. Actually pulled it on me and took a hostage."

"Headshot?"

"No, there was no clean angle. Shot him in the knee instead."

Joe nodded, and speared another bright-orange mockarrot with his fork. "Intentional?"

It annoyed me that he felt he had to ask that. "Well, yeah. I'm surprised the whole *city* didn't hear the drokker's screams."

My brother's only response was to nod again, his attention now back on the Lawbook in front of him.

"Joe, you *know* all this stuff. Why do you keep reading it?"

"The Law isn't fixed, Rico. We have to keep on top of it." He looked up, hitting me with that flinty gaze of his. "If we don't, then we might arrest someone for something that's no longer a crime, or let something go that now *is* a crime. You know that."

I started on my food. It was pasta in the shape of little Lawgivers; whoever had programmed chefbot that day had a strange sense of humour. "Yeah, yeah... It wouldn't do you any harm to relax now and then. Might even do you some good. Might make you a better Judge to be human. Look, we've got a lot of leave worked up already. Why don't we take a day off? We could get out of the city, go someplace where the predominant colour is green, not grey."

Judge Gibson dropped into the seat next to me. "I was thinking the same thing. Me and the guys have been talking about getting together sometime soon. You two in?"

"Yep," I said.

Joe asked, "Why?"

"Chew the fat," Gibson said. "Talk over old times."

"Old times? Gibson, we haven't been *alive* long enough to have old times. You guys are only twenty. And Rico and I are thirteen."

Gibson said, "Chronologically, yeah, but the geneticists sped up your aging, right? You've caught up with the rest of us." He sighed and shook his head. "And *you've* kept aging, Joe. You are *such* an old man. I remember the first time I met you guys. I was seven. We came into class one day and there you were, identical, sitting there looking like four- or five-year-olds." He laughed. "Me and Hunt, we used to give you such a hard time. Remember that?"

I said, "I remember that time when you spit in Little Joe's breakfast and he beat the snot out of you."

Gibson laughed harder. "I went running to Judge Duane, crying my eyes out. Man, that was funny."

Joe wasn't amused. "You were a bully. Nothing funny about that."

"Has he *ever* laughed?" Gibson asked me.

That got me thinking. Gibson and I wracked our brains. We did manage to recall a couple of occasions when Joe had smiled, but actually laughed? We couldn't think of a time when that had ever happened.

Half-way through the discussion, Joe got up and left. Anyone else, you might think he was pissed that we were talking about him right in front of his face. But Joe didn't get offended by things like this. He'd finished his meal, so it was time to go back on patrol.

But let's get back to Evan Quasarano. His gang kept their heads down, pretty much, for a couple of weeks, then someone robbed a local synthahol dispensary and all fingers were pointing at the Beadles.

I got the call on a Sunday evening, eighteen hundred hours, so first stop was Quasarano's apartment. It was a ground-floor place, Brendan Behan Block. The whole floor stank of sweat and grease and boiled vegetables. Ragged lumps of filth burst out of piles of damp garbage and squealed as they scattered ahead of me. They could have been oversized rats or undersized children—it was hard to tell.

The door to Quasarano's apartment opened before I could knock. He stepped out and pulled it closed behind him. "What do you want, Rico?"

"Is that any way to greet the man who's keeping you out of the cubes?" I nodded toward the door. "Anything you don't want me to see in there?"

His eyes narrowed. "You think me and the boys are responsible for turning over the boozery on Seventh, don't you? Wasn't us."

I stepped around him. "I'm gonna need to check inside, Quasarano."

"Rico... c'mon, man! I'm asking you as a friend. Don't do that."

It was hard not to smile at that. "A friend?" I placed my palm on the door. "Friendship goes both ways, kid. What have *you* ever done for *me*?"

"My mom's in there," he said quietly. "She doesn't know anything about... about anything. She thinks we're all angels."

I looked at him for a second, then pushed open the door. "I can be discreet, when I have to be."

Elizabeth Louise Quasarano was one of those women who are so deep into their fifties they look like they've got lost in there and they're never going to find their way out. She was stooped, frail, tiny—not even up to her son's shoulder. When she saw me, she almost dropped the casserole dish she was carrying toward the kitchen table. "Oh, sweet foetal Jovus! What's he done now?"

"Ma, it's okay," Quasarano said. "I'm not in trouble."

Mrs Quasarano regained her composure very quickly. "Right. Well, sit down. Both of you. There's enough to go around."

Staring at me from around the table were an old man who looked like he'd fought in the war and would bring it up in every conversation, Quasarano's two younger brothers, and his sister. The boys were twelve and eight, skinny but too tall for their clothes. The girl was nineteen, pretty but hollow-eyed, and seemed completely unsurprised to see me.

"I just need to ask Evan some questions, Mrs Quasarano. This won't take long."

She nodded. "Sit. And eat. Look at you—there's hardly a *pick* of meat on you."

Quasarano dragged over a chair, his brothers bunched up, and somehow I found myself taking off my helmet and gloves and sitting down, while Mrs Quasarano ladled the casserole into a small dish in front of me. "Uh, we're not really supposed to..."

"It's just a little goulash," she said. "Never hurt anyone. Better than that artificial rubbish you Judges eat. I don't know how you keep going. Thomas, be a good lad and pass the Judge some bread. No, don't use your hand! Pass him the *plate*. Grud above! Have I taught you nothing? I'm so sorry, Judge. I didn't raise my boys to be rude to guests."

She talked incessantly while we ate, telling me about the kids, her neighbours, her own childhood. No one else said a word; she never stopped long enough. At one point, I reached out to take the last bread roll and she slapped my hand. "In this home we *ask* before we take the last one. Where was I? Oh, right. So. My mother, Grud rest her, she was in the fashion industry. Well, that's what she *told* everyone, but between you and me, the truth is she worked in a clothing factory where she operated the machine that put buttons onto shirts. But she was a proud woman, very strict. Made sure we were brought up right..."

Eventually, the old man—Quasarano's paternal grandfather—pushed back his chair. "I'm done. Let the man ask Evan his questions, Liz. I'm sure he's got a whole backlog of innocent suspects to beat up."

Before the old man left the room, he pulled a litre bottle of Jepsom's Drunkifier from a cupboard. I didn't know much about booze, but I had a good idea of how much that bottle cost, and it was about as much as this whole family received from welfare in a month.

Quasarano paled at that, and looked away when I turned to him. "Your grandfather's right, Evan," I said. "You and I need to talk." I stood up and nodded to his mother. "Thank you for the meal, Mrs Quasarano. It was... tasty."

She beamed at that, and I moved toward the door before she could start talking again. "Evan?"

The kid followed me out into the apartment's narrow hallway, and closed the door behind him. He still wouldn't meet my gaze. "Rico, I'll get the boys to bring the booze and the money back to the store. Some of it's gone already, but..."

"Not them. Just you. And you weren't involved in the robbery. You found the stuff under the overpass. Got that? You don't know how it got there. You didn't keep it because you were scared that the Judges would blame you for taking it. If they offer you a reward—they probably won't—then you accept it. Don't pretend to be noble and decline it, all right? If you do, they'll become suspicious. In fact, if they *don't* offer you a reward, ask for one. Get annoyed if they say no."

He nodded. "Got it. Thanks, Rico."

I left him there in the hallway, and as I trudged my way through the garbage all I could think about was the meagre meal that his mother was happy to share with a stranger, and how Quasarano's brothers' and sister's clothes didn't fit.

I couldn't do much to help them, but I could do *something*. I pulled out my radio. "Control—Dredd."

"Go ahead, Dredd."

"Checked out the rumours of the Beadle gang's involvement in the synthahol robbery. Dead end. Looks like a rival gang's trying to shift the blame."

"Acknowledged, Dredd. We've got a 15-02 on the Westbound Narroway."

"On my way. And recommend you contact the owner of Brendan Behan Block. Damn place is knee-deep in garbage. That's a violation of city ordnance 4221. Tell him he's got twenty-four hours to get the block up to minimum standards, or he's looking at five in the cubes for neglect leading to possible endangerment."

That's how it began.

At my hearing, the investigators pinpointed that moment as "pivotal in Dredd's corruption." Their definition of "corrupt" didn't match mine, of course. Still doesn't.

Judge Rico Dredd became personally involved in the welfare of Evan Quasarano. Under the belief that he could steer the boy away from a life of crime, Dredd knowingly and deliberately covered up Quasarano's participation in a number of minor offences, one of which brought Dredd into contact with Quasarano's family.

Dredd was particularly impressed with Elizabeth Louise Quasarano, the boy's mother, and the manner in which she presided over her family and struggled to provide them with basic needs. Med-Judge Littman's psychological evaluation of Dredd suggests that Mrs Quasarano became a surrogate parent-figure, filling a void in the standard social structure that, as a clone raised in the Academy of Law, Dredd had never experienced.

Dredd personally intervened when Hector Quasarano, the boy's maternal grandfather, was arrested following a fracas involving three other war veterans. Dredd arranged for the charges against Hector Quasarano to be quashed, despite unequivocal evidence of Quasarano's willing participation in the event.

Though the defendant refuses to comment on this matter, we believe that it was around this time Dredd entered into a brief physical relationship with Stacie Quasarano, Evan's nineteen-year-old sister.

Stacie was quiet, thoughtful. The sort of girl that most guys wouldn't notice. And in truth I barely noticed her myself, the first few times I had dinner with the family. But one night, after the meal—I'd brought along a dozen re-Veal cutlets that I'd confiscated from a street-corner blackmarketeer—Stacie and I found ourselves sitting side-by-side on the sofa. Evan was out, the younger boys were in bed, and her mother and grandfather were taking the remaining cutlets to a neighbour.

It was a cold night, but I could feel the heat of Stacie's body even through my uniform. She wasn't saying much, just listening as I told her about my day.

I hadn't intended for it to happen. I hadn't intended for *any* of it to happen, of course. I used to call in to the Quasaranos' apartment maybe a couple of times a week. At first just to check on Evan, but soon it was because I liked it there. Most of the time the apartment was cold and damp, but the atmosphere was always warm and welcoming. The grandfather would tell stories about the war, and what America had been like back when it still *was* America. The kids would badger me with questions about being a Judge. Evan, too; I think he liked the idea, even though they were all far too old to sign up. Mrs Quasarano would tell me I was looking tired, or hungry. She'd fuss about me, making sure I was comfortable, giving me hot drinks. When I was leaving, she'd tell me to drive safely and not get into trouble. And one time, when I'd had a particularly tough day—a stolen truck had jack-knifed during a high-speed chase and killed Judge Ellard, who I'd known all my life—she could see that I was upset and she gave me a hug.

Stupid, I know. I was a Mega-City One Judge, trained in the best, toughest academy in the world. I shouldn't have cared. I didn't cry or anything like that, but this tiny woman wrapped her arms around me and told me that everything was going to be all right, and that meant more than any number of hours with a Department psychologist.

And so it happened. Stacie and I were the only ones awake in the apartment. I had a couple of hours free before my next shift. She was sitting next to me, her thigh pressed against mine as we watched some dumb game show on their crappy TV. We weren't even looking at each other, much. The sound was off and I was telling her how I'd chased down a perp.

Then Stacie's hand was on my leg. It seemed the most natural thing in the world to cover her hand with my own, to squeeze it a little and interlock our fingers.

She was the first girl I ever kissed. I didn't know what the hell I was doing, but I went with the flow.

Two

CELIBACY ISN'T EASY for most people. It's even tougher for Judges; there'll always be people out there who are drawn to power, and among them are those citizens willing to commit a crime just so that they'll be arrested.

In the Academy, we all had to pass a course called "Sexual Rebukes." It's not easy, and a good number of cadets utterly fail it. I like to imagine that they go on to have happier lives outside of the Department.

There are many reasons Judges can't have sex, and some of them are even credible. A Judge in a sexual relationship won't always have his or her mind on the job. That one makes sense, for most Judges. Despite the rumours, we're still human and detaching ourselves from our emotions isn't always easy. Then there's the danger of a Judge compromising a case by inadvertently revealing sensitive information to a lover, or of a perp hiring a hooker to seduce a Judge, filming the exciting parts, and embarking on a campaign of blackmail.

On top of all that, you really don't want a situation where some perp gets away with a crime because the Judge that might have stopped him is laid up in a med-centre with a dose of galloping crotch-rot.

They give other reasons, too, and some of them are less realistic.

When we were hitting puberty, Judge-Tutor Semple told us, "Sex makes babies. The city's already over-populated and under-resourced. The Department doesn't want to have to fund a nursery for the illegitimate offspring of you little drokkers. So keep it in your pants."

And then there was this classic, which me and Joe got from Judge Morphy: "We belong to the Justice Department. They own us, and everything about us. That includes any DNA samples we might be inclined to deposit inside another human being. So you have sex with someone and the Department will be well within its rights to charge them with receiving stolen goods." I still don't know whether Morphy was joking about that, or if he believed it.

The first time I realised that I was under suspicion was when Judge Ernest Kenner took me aside one day and said, "Rico. Need to talk to you about Stacie Quasarano."

I put on my best poker-face and denied all knowledge of the girl, but Kenner wasn't an idiot. He *knew* me: he'd run my final assessment. "It *ends*, Rico. Understood? I should report you, but, damn it, you've got the makings of a good Judge. So you get it out of your system and you end that relationship. And do it *right*. Let the girl down easy. You don't want her going to the local Sector House looking for you."

"All right," I said. "I'll do it."

"If you can't keep your libido in check, pay a visit to the med-unit and get a suppressant. Doesn't always work one hundred per cent, but it helps keep you focussed. If that fails, there's always surgery."

I'd heard that some Judges underwent castration as an alternative to self-control or drugs, but the idea sickened me. "I can control myself."

"I hope so, Rico. My advice? Sign up for a two-man team. It's a lot easier to resist temptation when there's another Judge around."

I thanked him for the advice and told him that I preferred to work alone. He seemed satisfied with that.

I applied for transfer to another part of the sector, and while I waited for that to come through I kept clear of the Quasarano family. Stacie had been getting kind of clingy anyway, always wanting to see me. I knew that I was better off without her, especially if Kenner was watching me.

That bugged me, though. Kenner had no call to interfere with my life, especially since I wasn't doing anything wrong. It was against the rules, yes, but that doesn't make it *wrong*.

ON THE WEST side of the sector there was what the politicians like to refer to as a "house of ill-repute." Joe and I received a call one morning, about seven months into our first year: someone had beaten the stomm out of one of the girls. They didn't call it in themselves, mind. A passing motorist saw the perp on the street, giving the victim the full treatment with his fists and feet.

By the time we got there, the usual localised amnesia epidemic had taken hold. No one could remember exactly what the John had looked like.

The brothel was run by a middle-aged woman calling herself Madam Ozelle. Big hair, more make-up than clothes, permanently suspicious. But she treated the girls well, made sure they were safe. "I might recognise him if he comes around again," she told me.

We were in the lobby of the small block, and the victim—twenty-two years old, attractive in a cheap kind of way—was curled up in an armchair nursing her injuries. She was being taken care of by one of her colleagues, who was appropriately dressed, though the nurse's outfit was far too small and much too shiny to be practical.

Joe said to Madam Ozelle, "You can't remember what he looks like, but you might recognise him? I'm not buying that. Withholding evidence is a crime, citizen. Let's go through it again. *Do* you know the assailant?"

"No, I do not."

I noticed the hesitation in her voice—and I knew that Joe'd spotted it too. I asked her, "Why didn't you report the assault?"

"We don't want any trouble, Judge. Sometimes it's best to say nothing."

"Well, you've *got* trouble," Joe said. "Six months, failure to report. Call it in, Rico."

"Joe, that won't help anyone." I stepped closer to the woman. "You know the assailant. But you're afraid of him. You run this place?"

She nodded, clearly trying not to swallow audibly.

"But you're not the owner."

Joe said, "Registered owner is Forest Patterson Dechant, aged fifty-five. Resident of Umesh Benison Block. Three priors, all for assault." Joe had checked out the place on the ride over: he was good at remembering details like that.

"So he's the one," I said, still staring at Madam Ozelle. "All you have to do is press charges and Dechant's looking at a minimum of two years for assault."

The girl on the armchair said, softly, "And then he'll get *out*."

Joe asked her, "How many times has he hit you?"

Her voice even softer, she said, "This is the first time. But about every couple of weeks he goes after one of us."

"Habitual," I said. "Your testimony is enough to warrant detention on suspicion. Joe?"

Joe nodded. "You finish up here. I'll take him in."

When he left, Madam Ozelle turned to me. "We're still not going to press charges against him, Judge." She gave the young woman a nasty look, then added, "Bad as Dechant is, we *need* him. Our clients know what he's like. They treat us as well as they do only because they're scared of him."

"Your input is no longer a requirement, citizen." I nodded to the injured girl. "Her statement is enough. Joe will encourage a confession out of Dechant."

"It's not just that... The other houses around here, well, most of them have a Dechant of their own. It kind of goes with the territory. As soon as they learn that he isn't around, they'll come here, start trying to poach my girls. And not by offering them a bigger cut. More like, 'Come with us and you won't get maimed.'"

"Not really my problem, citizen. You need to hire better security."

That night, four thugs engaged by a rival brothel showed up, armed with obvious intentions and hidden guns. They barged through the place, kicking open doors and scaring the clientele.

Until they kicked open the *wrong* door. The door that had me waiting behind it.

The first guy was a bruiser. Fifty years old, ex-military. Knew how to fight and an expert at intimidation. I punched him in the throat, slammed my boot into his left knee as he staggered back, finished him with an elbow to the solar plexus.

The other three were no fools: they were already running before the bruiser spewed his guts onto the room's cheap carpet. They were maybe ten metres from the stairs leading down to the building's main entrance. They didn't make it.

They didn't know I was a Judge. I was off-duty, wearing civilian clothes. All they knew was that they'd got their butts handed to them by someone a lot younger, smarter, stronger and faster. They wouldn't be coming back.

First thing I did, after I hauled the thugs out of Madam Ozelle's place and watched them crawl, limp and bleed their way back to their crappy pick-up truck, was pay a visit to the brothel that had hired them.

I made it plain to the man in charge that his actions would not be tolerated in future. Four broken fingers and several shattered windows later, he was very much in agreement with me. And then, when he realised I was a Judge, he offered to make "financial reparations": a thousand credits not to arrest him.

I brought the money back to Madam Ozelle. She said, "But you should keep it. You earned it."

"Judges don't need money," I told her. "Use it to pay for the repairs, and to clean up."

The woman regarded me for a few seconds. "But... you won't *always* be a Judge. You'll need money when you retire, won't you?"

That caught me off-guard. I had never considered that one day I might no longer be a Judge. I realised that it was actually possible that at some point in my future—assuming that I wasn't killed on duty—I might decide to just quit.

In all my years in the Academy of Law, I don't think that I had even once asked myself, "What would I like to be, if not a Judge?" Judging was all I had been trained for, all I knew. I was Judge Rico Dredd, the best of a new breed of Judges. Mega-City One's finest. And I enjoyed being a Judge. Hell, I *loved* it. It was intense and relentless and unbelievably dangerous.

But was it *forever*?

Judges who quit are usually forced out by injury, or, in a small number of cases, old age. Either way, they just can't cut it any more.

They're given a choice: teach at the Academy, work behind the scenes at Control, or take the Long Walk. That last one's a death sentence: they're supplied with guns, ammo and rations, and sent out to dispense justice in the Cursed Earth, or the undercity, or the Black Atlantic.

I'd always been aware of those options, but, now that I thought about it, I realised that I didn't like any of them. I couldn't see myself half-blind or maimed, limping through the corridors of the Academy and yelling at the cadets, or sitting behind a wall of monitors operating the spycams and guiding younger Judges through arrests.

Nor did I want to end up as some emaciated, self-righteous nomad choking on irradiated dust, trying to bring Big City Law to a decaying town where the wiser inhabitants have long since bought themselves a copper-cased ticket to oblivion.

Still, I didn't keep the money. I'd nowhere to put it, for a start. Judges don't have bank accounts.

Madam Ozelle said, "Well, you need *some* sort of reward. That's only fair." She turned to one of the girls. "Amber?"

Three

It was what the psychologists called my "inevitable slide into corruption." A couple of nights a week I'd check on Madam Ozelle's place, just to make sure everything was in line. Yes, I usually spent an hour or so with Amber or one of the other girls while I was there, but that was just a bonus. The real reason I was there was to keep the peace.

And keeping the peace sometimes meant dispensing the violence. The owner of another local establishment took exception to the situation—she didn't like the idea of a brothel where the employees got to keep most of their own money—so I had to sort her out, too.

Ambrosia Cropper. Mid-sixties, face like something that would turn even a marine biologist's stomach. She came crashing in to Madam Ozelle's place with three sons and four grandsons, all armed with rockball bats, steel knuckles and a pair of ancient sawn-off shotguns. One of her sons said, "We're takin' over!" and that was the last thing anyone ever heard him say, apart from the screams, and they didn't last long. That's what you get when you're stupid enough to pull a gun on a Judge. I left the rest of them alive, but nursing a good collection of fractures, breaks and dislocations. Cropper and I came to an understanding: she'd treat her own girls—and boys—better, and she'd donate a quarter of her take to

Madam Ozelle. In return, I wouldn't arrest her and dismantle her entire operation.

I arranged for Madam Ozelle to hire three new security guys. They weren't the smartest, but they were smart enough to know that they should keep their heads down, and never mention my involvement to any other Judges. I made it clear to them what would happen otherwise.

Two were ex-military, both dishonourably discharged for "unruly conduct unbecoming a member of the armed forces." In other words, they had a tendency to settle disputes with their fists. That was why I chose them. In a place like that, you want the bouncers to quickly gain a no-nonsense reputation.

The third guy we hired was Evan Quasarano. He was still only seventeen, but even at that age he was bigger than me. He was a good brawler, and scared enough of me to follow orders. And he knew the streets and the sort of vermin who slithered through them.

It was not a nice part of the sector. On patrol, we'd encounter more—considerably more—dust-heads and drunks than sober citizens. Some of the older Judges ran a weekly book on who'd find the most bodies. Apparently, the Resyk truckers used to fight over the routes through the area, because their bonuses depended on the number of stiffs they brought in.

The district was home to low-rent data hackers and unlicensed medicians, document forgers and counterfeiters, bootleggers and head-wreckers. There were gambling dens, black markets and mobster hideouts.

My job as a Judge was to clean it up, but of course that was impossible if I only played within the rules. For years, Judges had patrolled the sector without making a dent in the crime levels, because in a place like that, if citizens see a Judge coming, they suddenly lose their memories and their ability to speak and even the most highly-feared local ganglords become beatified.

So my approach was to take the fight to *their* level. Be seen as one of them. Pretty soon, everyone who believed they were important got to know my name. Judge Rico Dredd can be bought, that's what they learned. I'd bust a backroom bookie, scare the crap out of his punters, and he'd beg me to let it slide. A stuffed envelope would somehow find its way into my hands, and I'd let him off with a warning.

Because what's the point in imprisoning a guy for something that—let's be honest here—is mostly a victimless crime? I send him to the cubes, that costs the city at least sixty thousand credits a year. But if I leave him with a warning, make it clear to him that his actions will only be tolerated to a point, then he's out there still running his little games and keeping his punters too busy to get into any real trouble. If someone's spending his day playing nine-card wallaby or making half-cred bets on snail-races, then he's not murdering his wife or heading to the bank to make a shotgun withdrawal.

Same with the gangs and the mobsters. I got to know them, explained to them that if they kept their heads down, they got to keep those heads. The mobs controlled the district's protection rackets. I didn't like that, but I tolerated it. It's hard enough for the average citizen to afford insurance; the big, reputable companies won't insure anyone who doesn't have much in the way of assets. But the mobs didn't care about background credit checks and payment histories. Say there's some corner-store owner who's plagued with kleptos, vandals and gangs of flash-mobbing juves; well, there's no way he can afford real insurance. But he pays the mob a couple of hundred each month, and they take care of him. They make sure that the local thugs and spug-heads understand that the store is off-limits. The owner mightn't like paying protection money—and sure as stomm stinks, he doesn't want to ever miss a payment—but he's in a better position than he would be otherwise. He doesn't have to replace stolen or damaged stock, and no-one's going to ram-raid his store if the consequences involve lead pipes and kneecaps.

The mobs ran the loan-sharks, too, and it was pretty much the same deal. Sure, their interest rates were exorbitant, but it was the only way the average citizen could get hold of some quick cash.

What I'm getting at is that most mob-run districts actually have less crime, and are a lot safer, than they would be if the Judges ever managed to get rid of the mobs. The mobs bring order. It might not be the kind of order we'd like, but it's better than chaos.

So the mob-bosses got to know me, and I made sure they didn't step out of line. I didn't tell them outright what I was doing, because that wouldn't work. You can't go up to a guy like Sparks Petrosky and start laying down rules: you'd end up occupying several widely-spaced buckets. So you get him thinking that you're working for him.

I'd meet Petrosky about every ten days. Sometimes he'd point the finger at someone causing trouble in the district, and I'd arrest the creep—had to keep my numbers up; I didn't want Justice Central figuring out what I was doing—and that would make things better for everyone. Now and then, I'd have to confront Petrosky about his own guys being too heavy-handed, like if maybe they came down too hard on a guy who owed them money and he wound up dead.

I'd tell him, "Justice has to be *seen* to be done, Sparks. So you hand over one of your boys—someone low on the totem pole, if you want, I don't care who—and I'll put him away for a five-stretch for involuntary manslaughter." Petrosky would quibble, but eventually I'd get my way.

I guess, from an outsider's point of view, what I was doing probably *did* look like corruption. But the Council of Five and the Chief Judge weren't out there on the streets with the rest of us, wading through the filth. They sat in their polished throne-rooms with their unblemished uniforms and made decisions about the lives of ordinary citizens they'd never met.

Well, I'd met those citizens. I lived among them. I protected them—from outsiders *and* from themselves—and I understood what it meant to be a Judge. Every decision we made affected people's lives. We gun down an opportunistic burglar, that's one creep off the streets. But what about his family? Suppose he was stealing because it was the only way he could make enough money to keep them fed and housed? The official system treated the symptoms, not the disease.

My way was better. I've always believed that, always will. I consorted with criminals because they're people too. It's just human nature to covet what we don't have. The solution is not tighter laws, but a clearer demonstration of consequences. Education, not incarceration.

I was *among* the people I'd been trained to Judge, not above them. Working with them, not against them. The other Judges were lion-tamers where I was a shepherd, if you see what I mean. And if I made some money on the side, so what? It didn't distract me from my job. If anything, the money was an incentive to keep going. Each credit was a token that proved I was going in the right direction.

I HAD MY guys on the streets keeping an eye on things. They told me what was going down with the gangs and the solo low-lifes. That's how I got word that Judge Kenner had been snooping again.

Kenner was coming into the sector when I wasn't around, talking to people. Asking them about me. But he hadn't approached me directly, and that's what worried me.

So I had Petrosky's hackers check him out, see exactly what he was up to. Turned out I was right to worry: Kenner was building a case against me, trying to find solid proof that I'd gone off-book. I had the hackers check out Kenner's arrest record, too... His numbers were down; he'd spent so much time investigating me, he was neglecting his beat.

That wasn't good. Even if Kenner himself couldn't find any evidence—and I'd covered myself pretty well—then it was only a matter of time before someone else in the Department wondered what he was up to. If they investigated *him*, that would lead them to me.

I couldn't let that happen. Ernest Kenner was a good Judge, but he was old-school. He was rigid in his understanding and application of the Law. One of us had to go, and I didn't plan on it being me.

Besides, he'd already been a Judge for a long time. He was hitting forty; his best years were probably behind him. A Judge gets old, he gets slow. Starts making bad decisions. Like investigating a younger Judge when he should be spending his time dealing with real perps.

I took a pragmatic approach and weighed up the options. I could stop what I was doing and toe the line—though that wouldn't be easy, what with everything I'd already set in motion—or I could retire Kenner. In the long run, he'd be just another Judge. He'd make a tiny difference to the city as a whole. But me, I was poised to make a *huge* difference.

It wasn't an easy decision, but it had to be done. I contacted

Kenner—off the record, of course—and let him think I was Joe. Told him, "It's about Rico."

"What about Rico?" he asked.

"I'm not sure, sir. He... He seems just different, these days. And I've been hearing things... Rumours about excessive violence. Complaints about his off-duty behaviour."

The old fool agreed to meet me to talk and see what we could do about the situation before the Department had to be brought in.

I had to do it. It was him or me.

We met at the old turnpike at the edge of the atomic wastelands. The radiation from the rad-pits interfered with the public surveillance cameras, and made radio transmissions difficult to track.

Kenner showed up on time. Strode toward me with his hand extended. "Joe."

"Wrong."

I didn't shoot him. Bullets can sometimes be traced, and even when they *can't*, the fact that he'd been shot would immediately steer the investigation in a direction I didn't want it to go.

So I put him into a rad-pit.

Kenner didn't die quickly, or quietly, and I regret that. I didn't want him to suffer. Despite everything that's been said about me, I'm not a cruel man.

My spies told me that he was reported missing a day later. The Public Surveillance Unit tracked his movements through the city right up to the edge of the wastelands, and a week of pit-dredging turned up what remained of his body.

Petrosky's hackers wiped Kenner's file on me. He'd never logged his suspicions, never spoken to anyone. There was nothing to tie his death to me.

I was free and clear.

Four

I GOT MY own apartment. Not unusual for a Judge. It got me closer to the action, set me deeper among the people.

The investigation into my actions said I was "building a criminal empire," but that's plainly stomm. It wasn't an empire. It was me on my own, bringing order to the chaos. Sometimes things turned sour, that's bound to happen. Some people died, like Judge Kenner, but no one can deny that—thanks to me—more people *lived.*

Serious crimes were down in my district, *way* down, and that was because the citizens trusted me. Or they knew me, which amounted to the same thing. One time, a dealer moved in with a batch of high-grade endorphium. He approached Petrosky, tried to come to an arrangement where he'd sell the stuff and give Petrosky a good-sized cut.

Petrosky came to me, I arrested the perp, and the endorphium was seized and destroyed. Well, most of it. It's actually a very useful drug; pumps up the user's energy levels, keeps him sharp, keeps him going long after anyone else would have quit. I kept a small supply on me, just in case I was ever in a bind and really needed a boost. But the point is, Sparks Petrosky turned in that dealer and cut himself out of a huge chunk of money, all because he understood that was how the game was now played.

I knew what I was doing, and I was doing it well. A newly-paroled perp moved into the district, or a new gang, and I'd pay them a visit. It's a process, really. Almost an algorithm. You arrive unannounced, kick in the door, take down whatever muscle they have, and make it clear that if they want to operate in the area then there's a tax. And they play their part, too: they react with indignation and threats, you bust a few more heads—or even, if you really have to hammer home the point, you find the guy's second-in-command and you put a slug inside his skull. That one usually makes them realise that you're not messing around.

It's not like it's *murder* to kill a henchman, though my prosecution made it clear that they didn't agree with that. They were wrong, and they'd have known that if they'd been riding Lawmasters instead of desks. Like I said, it's an algorithm, an equation. A dead second-in-command perp is a lot better than a dead innocent citizen. And of course they'd never stop at just *one* dead citizen, so whichever way you look at it, my method saved lives.

So, yeah, my body-count was up, reported crime was down, and I figured that would be enough to keep the Department's nose out of my business. But I was wrong. It all came crashing down.

Thanks to my brother.

HE'D BEEN SUSPICIOUS of me for a long time, but hadn't said anything, so I didn't know. Joe was like that; the ultimate poker-face. You almost never knew what he was thinking.

He showed up at my place one day. This was my second apartment, a nice place. I was on the roof, enjoying the sun.

Joe strode across the rooftop straight for me, like he was approaching a perp, and I knew what was coming. I also knew that I could cope with it. I'd always been smarter than him. Maybe not academically, but I had the street-smarts that he lacked.

"You're out of uniform," he said.

"Day off. We *are* entitled to time off. You'd know that if you ever *took* it. What do you want?"

"Been checking your stats. Body-count's giving me cause for suspicion, and you've got an above-average number of complaints."

That bugged me. A lot. He had no right to pry into the way I ran things. And I knew that he didn't come up with it on his own. Kenner was still pretty fresh in my mind, and I didn't want things to have to go that way again. "So the bigwigs sent Little Joe to give Big Rico a *lecture*, huh?"

He stopped in front of me, scowled down. "You're drunk, Rico."

I'd had a couple of drinks. Not more than two. I was in no way drunk. And certainly sober enough to hold my own in a battle of wits with him.

Amber came out onto the patio. "Everythin' all right, honey?"

"Just my other half come to give me some earache," I told her. "Better leave us be, honey. Little Joe can be real *mean* when he takes a mind."

Joe looked around. At the pool, the expensive planters, the fifteen-hundred-cred Taneasy lounger I was lying on. "Where did you get the money for all this?"

I said, "Wouldn't you like to know?" I hadn't meant to say that. I'd always planned that if anyone asked I'd say that the apartment belonged to some rich guy who was spending a year in Texas City, and he'd asked me to live there so that it wouldn't get burgled. But Joe was pissing me off. Or maybe I was drunker than I'd thought.

"It's got to *stop*, Rico! You can't keep breaking the rules!"

I put down my drink. "I do what I want. I'm a Judge—I *make* the rules." Yeah, I guess I *was* heading toward wasted by that stage. Part of me was thinking, *Shut the drokk up, Rico!* but Joe's holier-than-everyone attitude had long since lost its charm. He was turning into a self-assured scuzzball who'd forgotten which of us had received the higher marks in the Academy. Or maybe he *hadn't* forgotten; maybe it had stuck in his craw, and it was all he could think about. I said to him, "I say the word..." I snapped my fingers. "Boom. You're *gone*. So don't tell big brother what to do, Joey."

I'd meant that as a joke. I mean, he was my brother, he knew I'd never actually threaten him. Or he *should* have known. If he'd had a personality, he'd have been able to tell that I wasn't really serious.

Joe reached out and grabbed the collar of my shirt, hauled me up so we were face to face. "Get this through your head. You're *not* my big brother. You never were. You're *me* and there's something wrong with you! *Do* something—or I will."

He shoved me back into the Taneasy and stormed away.

Joe had kept his helmet on, but I didn't need to see his eyes to know what he was thinking.

He was scared. He saw that I'd strayed from the rigid path set out by the Academy, and he knew that he wouldn't be able to keep up. He wasn't prepared for the way the department would have to change if it was to keep control of the city.

A government can exist only as long as the people allow it. You might say, "Yeah? What about a dictatorship?" Well, the same rule applies. Dictators can only push so far before they're overthrown.

And that's what Mega-City One became when the Judges took over. There's no democracy, but then most democracies are that in name only: the citizens are allowed to choose their figurehead, but the people with the power remain the same. The elections make a difference to the citizens' lives in the same way that changing a hood ornament makes a difference to a car's destination.

Mega-City One's Justice Department was established by my clone-father, Eustace Fargo, as a way to return order to the chaos after a succession of devastating wars. It worked, too, for a while. But sooner or later every empire falls. The smart people either try to steer that fall, or they get the hell out of the way.

Joe was part of the establishment and it bothered him that I was able to stand outside of it, to see the cracks as they appeared. He would take me down, if the opportunity showed itself. And he knew that he could do it a lot easier and faster if he were prepared to break the rules, but if he did that, then he wouldn't be Judge Joe Dredd. Then he'd be just like everyone else.

JOE'S SUSPICIONS WERE confirmed when a routine speeder chase took him into my patch. The driver was just a kid. Fifteen years old. Young enough to still believe that he was indestructible and smarter than everyone else, and tall enough to be able to see over the steering-wheel.

The kid blazed through a red light coming off the elevated highway, and next thing a Lawmaster was roaring up behind, lights flashing. If he'd been smart, he'd have pulled over, grovelled an apology and silently prayed for a lenient term. But he was an idiot—he tried to outrun Joe Dredd.

The stolen car—a '78 Fellini convertible, with deep red bodywork and fitted with a state-of-the-art hover-plate that allowed it to reach several hundred KPH—ended up embedded in a wall. The kid died, of course, his skull coming to a stop a lot later than the rest of his body, but that was no loss. Just natural selection in action.

But as Joe was waiting for a clean-up crew and trying to keep the Lookie-Lous away, he was approached by one of my guys, Evan Quasarano. Understand that I don't know for sure this is *exactly* how it went down—I had to piece it together from a couple of reports and a few things I heard—but the outcome was the same.

"Hey, JD," Quasarano said. He'd taken to calling me that, instead of using my first name; you don't let people know you're friends with a Judge.

Joe nodded to him. "What can I do for you, citizen?"

Quasarano peered past him at the wreckage. "What happened here?"

"None of your concern. Move along before I cite you for obstruction."

Quasarano laughed at that. "Yeah, right. Listen, old man Petrosky sent one of his guys over last night. They want to talk to you about some trouble they're having with Vijay McMorran and his crew. Figure it's the usual, you know? Pushing past the edges of their territory."

Now, my brother might be a cold-hearted, humourless, unimaginative, by-the-book stickler for rules, but he's not an idiot. Far from it. It was clear to him that Quasarano thought they knew each other, and that could only mean he thought Joe was me. And why wouldn't he? We looked the same, sounded the same, wore the same badge. So Joe played along to find out more. "Got it," he said. "So how did things go last night, anyway?"

"Pretty quiet. No trouble. Well, there was one guy who claimed he wasn't satisfied and he wanted his money back, but we took care of it."

"Glad to hear it. What did you do with him?"

"The usual."

"You get his ID? I might want to pay him a visit myself."

Quasarano nodded. "Sure, yeah. Name's Donald Fletta. Old guy. Maybe forty or fifty, or sixty. Lives over in the Crimson Furrows. You know it?"

"Yeah, I know it," Joe said. "Fletta still in one piece?"

"A few bruises and cuts, that's all. Like you always say, right? You can only take money off a dead man once."

"That's true," Joe told him. He gestured back toward the crowd. "Better get clear. Med-wagon's coming in. What you said about Petrosky...? He mention a time when we're supposed to meet?"

"No. Guess he wants you to call him to arrange it."

"Good work. Thanks, kid."

And Evan Quasarano smiled and nodded and felt pleased with himself, and wandered back into the crowd without the slightest inkling of what he had just set in motion.

Five

I SHOULD GO back a bit, I think; I'm getting ahead of myself. You see, the whole deal with guys like Sparks Petrosky was that they thought I was working for them, when really they were working for me. I got them to temper their actions—no more murdering innocents if it could be avoided, for example—and they got a certain amount of freedom. Together, we established an uneasy sort of peace. I let them run their protection, prostitution, drug-dealing and loan-sharking with the understanding that they didn't do anything too flashy that might draw the wrong sort of attention. You could say that I was acting as an unofficial intermediary between the criminal classes and the judiciary.

They gave me a cut, sure, because if I hadn't taken it they would have been suspicious. And I'm not going to lie, the money was nice. In the Academy, we were raised without luxuries of any kind. There were no soft pillows or foaming baths, no rich foods or pet dogs or birthday presents. No hugs from Mom, no stories at bedtime, no games or toys and not many jokes. We didn't get to have a real childhood. We didn't get to have an adolescence, either. No girlfriends or boyfriends, no staying out late and sneaking home just before dawn, no concerts or movie theatres or parties or any of that.

No *fun*. Judges are expected to sit in judgement on the ordinary people without really knowing what it's like to *be* a person.

So I'd decked out my apartment with the latest in cool gadgets and stocked the refrigerator with treats. I rented movies and bought music and dated girls and sometimes got drunk or high and enjoyed myself.

But my new life didn't come free. The price was that I had to do some things that were technically illegal. I had to be seen to be just as bad as Sparks Petrosky and the others believed me to be.

And that meant, sometimes, doing little bad things in order to prevent larger bad things from happening. It's a matter of scale, and that's what Joe could never understand.

Virgil Livingstone was a small-time dealer who worked on the fringes of the district. He had a four-hours-a-week job delivering office supplies, and the uniform gave him access to a lot of places where he'd otherwise stand out.

He sometimes sold weapons or banned publications, but he mostly dealt low-impact drugs like cane sugar, caffeine, snizz or crawbies. And every now and then he'd come into contact with someone who could get hold of endorphium or even powdered jetsam. He sold to the city's fairly-rich and mildly-famous; mostly k-list celebrities and the kids of declining corporate empires.

And Livingstone and I had an arrangement. He told me who he was selling to, and I didn't arrest him. See, if I *had* arrested him, then his clients would have just bought their stuff from someone else. But with him free to deal, I was able to build a very nice dossier on the corrupt elements in the mid-to-high levels of Mega-City One society.

He didn't know what I was really doing, of course. He saw me as an enforcer who collected the tribute for Petrosky, so it was vital that I played that role with conviction. That meant that sometimes I had to hurt him.

For weeks, he'd been putting me off; "I've *got* the money, but I just don't have it *on* me." I let that slide. I knew from my other contacts that he was actually telling the truth. A large shipment of quality European chocolate was coming in across the Black Atlantic, and I wanted to wait until it was in before I made my move. I could arrest the buyers as well as the dealers and *really* make an impact.

And then the rumours started to spread that the shipment already *had* come in, that Virgil Livingstone was now starting to think that he was big enough to sell it without Sparks getting his cut.

So I had to teach him a lesson, plain and simple. It had to be a lesson he'd never forget.

VIRGIL LIVINGSTONE'S OFFICE door opened and he grinned nervously at me. "Hey, Rico. Good timing. I was just going to see you, man. I got—"

"I hear you've been holding out on me, Virgil."

"What? No! No way! See, what happened was there were these guys who—"

He stopped then, staring down the barrel of my Lawgiver.

"You're three weeks late with the payment, Virgil. Hand it over. You've got four seconds."

"Okay, okay... I've got it here." Slowly, carefully, he moved his hand inside his jacket. "That's what I was trying to *tell* you." He pulled out a thick, plastic-wrapped bundle of cash. "Eighteen grand, Rico. I know that's less than I owe, but that's because I did a deal that got..." He stopped talking, just stared at me as he held out the bundle of cash. "Rico... Please..."

"Eighteen's not enough. You're disrespecting the situation, Livingstone. You're disrespecting *me*. What was your mark-up on the deal? Fifty per cent? Sixty? I want all of it."

He slowly shook his head. "No. Look, I did make a profit. Nothing like fifty per cent, though. That's what I'm trying to say, if you just let me *finish*. I sold the chocolate at a knock-down price because there's another shipment coming in, a much larger one. Two months, and we'll have the clients crying for more. I'm thinking we can quadruple the price, and they'll pay it. You see what I'm saying? Rico, this is the deal of a *lifetime!* This eighteen grand"—again, he waved the cash in front of my face—"is all I made on the first deal. That's all I've got."

I took the cash and weighed up my options. It sounded like a good deal, and Livingstone was too scared of me to lie. But I couldn't just leave it there. Something like this new deal should have been run past Sparks and me first.

But because he didn't do that, because he was trying to bump up his own status, Livingstone had to be taught a lesson. I grabbed him by the collar, forced him down to his knees.

One good scare is usually all it takes. I held my Lawgiver right in front of his face, side-on, so he could see the ammo-selector. "You see *this*, you sweat-soaked bag of stomm? Incendiary. You know what that round can do to a human head at point-blank?"

"Jovus! Rico, *please...*"

I flipped the gun's selector. "Or maybe you'd prefer a Ricochet, huh? Bounces around in your skull. You'll be dead in seconds, but they'll be the longest seconds you can imagine."

I'd used this trick before. It scares the hell out of the perps, makes sure they stay in-line. You let them *think* they're getting a Standard Execution shot when really you flip it back to Ricochet. Afterwards, they're so grateful to be alive that it'd take something really drastic to shatter their new-found loyalty.

"You don't like that, Livingstone? That's not how you want to go? Okay. Fast and simple." I flipped the selector. "See that? Standard Execution. That more your style?"

"Rico, show some mercy! Please!"

"This *is* drokkin' mercy, punk!" I yelled at him "This is me being lenient, doing it painlessly. More than you deserve. You knew the rules, but you tried to go it alone. Now you pay."

Livingstone was crying now. "I'll give you everything I get on the new deal! *Everything!* My entire profit!"

Gotcha, I thought. *You're mine now, creep. Forever.* After this, I'd be able to tell him to jump from the top of Power Tower, and he'd do it.

And then *he* was there, coming out of the shadows. Joseph Dredd. My brother.

"Step away from him, Rico. Now."

So Joe had been following me. Maybe he'd picked up a trick or two on the streets, because I'd had no idea.

A thousand thoughts ran through my head. I was fast, definitely faster than Joe, and my gun was already drawn. He wouldn't be expecting it. I figured I had a good chance of taking him out.

But if I did, then what? I didn't know who he'd told, or if another

Judge had ordered him to watch me. If a Judge goes missing, the Department turns the city upside-down looking for him. Like they did with Kenner. They'd investigate me, if I wasn't already on their watch-lists, and they'd find out everything. There was no way I could convince them that I was doing the right thing.

Joe stepped closer, his hands empty. I still had time.

And there was still a way out of this.

I said to him, "I was wondering when you'd show up, Little Joe."

Livingstone muttered something under his breath about "two of them!" but although I was looking at him, my attention was on Joe.

"You're not going to let this rest, are you, little brother? Okay. Two ways it can go. Either we work together—or one of us doesn't leave here alive."

He said nothing, as I'd expected.

"Which is it to be, Joe? Stick with me, I'll show you how to become a very rich man."

Joe said, "I've seen all I want to see, Rico."

He needs a demonstration, I remember thinking. *Have to show him what this is really all about.* Aloud, I said, "No, Joe. I don't think you have. You haven't seen what happens to scum who don't do what I say!" I pointed my gun at Livingstone's chest, aimed down at his sternum. I'm a good shot; I knew exactly what damage a Ricochet bullet would do at that range, at that angle. Crack the bone, lodge in the body. He'd be out of commission for a few days. A good demonstration to Livingstone *and* to Joe.

Livingstone started to back away. "Please, Rico. I can't pay you any more!"

I smirked. "You'll pay with your life, then!" I squeezed the trigger.

I knew the instant that the gun fired that something was wrong. You develop an instinct for that in the Academy. Different rounds have different kickbacks. This one...

This one was *not* a Ricochet bullet. It was Standard Execution.

Joe's fault, damn him. Totally his fault. He'd distracted me before I could reselect Ricochet.

Livingstone collapsed face-down to the floor, a growing pool of blood spreading out from under him.

Out of habit, I dropped down into a crouch next to him, checked his pulse, even though I knew there was no point: the exit wound in his back was large enough to put my fist in.

I looked up at Joe. He was staring at me like he couldn't believe what he'd just seen.

I could barely believe it myself. I'd killed before, plenty of times, but that was always intentional. It wasn't like this. But there are no take-backs with a Lawgiver. There's no "Undo" button on a gun.

If I'd been anyone else, Joe would already have shot me. No, scratch that—he'd have shot me *before* I pulled the trigger on Livingstone.

"This... this doesn't have to be a problem, Joe!"

He said nothing, just slowly crouched and pulled out his Lawgiver from his boot-holster.

"We can make it look like an accident!"

Joe straightened up, still staring at me. "No way, Rico. I'm taking you in."

I wanted to make him understand. Had to make him see that my way was right. Why *couldn't* he see that? We were the same person!

He swapped his gun to his left hand. He's pretty much ambidextrous—as am I—but the left hand was important. He wasn't quite ready to gun me down.

Or maybe, I thought, *he knows he* can't *do it.*

"*You* take *me?*" I said. "Don't make me laugh! I was *always* better!" I wanted Joe to see reason here. Livingstone was scum. He'd have died on the streets long ago if it hadn't been for me. His death today was an accident. And it was more than he deserved.

But my brother—that humourless, stick-in-the-mud, festering *scab*—just stared me down.

All right, then, I thought. *He's not going to budge. He's going to make me do it. He's going to make me draw on him. If that's what it takes to get out of this, then fine. I could kill him and then switch the scene around a little, make it look like it was* me *who'd stumbled across* him *attempting to extort money from Livingstone.* But no, if I was already under investigation, they'd know not to trust me.

But if they caught me... I knew what happened to corrupt Judges. *Better to die here and now than to end up like that.*

And then a simpler thought occurred: *I could just kill Joe and pretend that he's me and I'm him.* They'd never be able to tell. Physically we're identical, right down to our DNA. I'd just have to get used to people calling me Joe instead of Rico. And if there were any discrepancies, like if I didn't know something that Joe was expected to know, then I'd be able to cover that by pretending I was in shock at having had to kill my own brother.

"Too bad, Little Joe," I said to him. "But *one* of us has to go."

"You're not going to shoot me," he said.

That's where I made a mistake, and who can blame me? He was my brother. I thought he meant that I wasn't willing to shoot him—which would have been dead wrong on his part—but he actually meant I wasn't going to be *able* to shoot him. Turned out he was right about that.

He stood staring at me, Lawgiver by his side, not moving.

"Damn you, Joe, fire!"

Nothing. Not even a flicker of a reaction.

I raised my gun. "Why don't you *fire*—?"

He rushed at me, moving faster than I was expecting. I pulled the trigger three times before a blinding pain in my jaw sent me flying backwards.

For a long time, I didn't know how he did it. How could he have moved so fast? How could I have *missed*—I was always the better shot, always faster on the draw. In the Academy, he never once beat me.

But he took me down without firing a shot, got barely a scratch in return.

Eventually, I figured out how he managed it, but of course by then it was far too late. It wasn't that Joe was better than me. I was always the best, and I still am. It was *because* I'm the best.

It was subconscious. I *let* him do it because I couldn't kill my own brother. He was part of me.

That's the only explanation that makes sense. See, Joe was well within the Law to kill me, but he didn't. He used his fists instead of his trigger-finger, because it was the same for him. He couldn't kill a part of himself.

Six

THERE WAS NO trial, of course, but there was an official investigation, and that was almost the same thing.

They kept me cuffed, gagged and under mild sedation while witnesses were brought in, scanned, questioned, cross-questioned, and dismissed. Few of the witnesses would look me in the eye, or even glance in my direction.

I'd tried to explain what I'd been doing. I showed them the dossier I'd compiled on Sparks Petrosky and the other mob leaders. I gave them the names of the losers, users and abusers I'd encountered. And I did a damn good job. Anywhere else, they'd have understood. They'd probably have pinned a Grud-damned *medal* on me.

But none of it made any difference. I'm sure they went out and made all the appropriate arrests afterwards, but the investigation was really about one thing: punishing me because I'd tried to make a difference. Because I'd rocked the system. Because I'd shown them a better way, and made them look bad in the process.

The Justice Department exists because they have the only voice in the city. They're untouchable, unimpeachable. They wield absolute power over the citizens. And they hung me out to dry because I showed them how tenuous their position really is. I was an embarrassment to them because I was *right*.

On the evening of the third day, at the hearing's closing session,

I said nothing; there was nothing left to say. I could have protested my innocence one more time, but that would have been pointless. They wanted me gone, and there was nothing I could do about that.

And then I was instructed to stand.

Chief Judge Clarence Goodman looked down at me and hesitated for a moment. "Rico Dredd, on the charge of the premeditated murder of citizen Virgil Alain Livingstone, this board has taken your testimony, witness statements and the physical evidence into consideration. We have concluded that citizen Livingstone's death was unintentional, and on said charge this board finds you innocent."

A murmur broke out among the gathered Judges, and for a moment I almost believed that I'd be exonerated. But I knew better. I knew how the Justice Department worked.

Goodman waited for the noise to subside. "But Livingstone's death was not unavoidable. Rico Dredd, you abused your position as a Judge for personal gain, and in doing so you put the life of citizen Livingstone—and countless others—at risk. A Judge's first duty is to serve the citizens, and in that duty you have failed."

I looked around. Joe was there, standing at the back with his arms folded, looking only at Goodman. Next to him was Gibson, but at least *he'd* had the decency to remove his helmet and appear concerned for his old friend.

"Rico Dredd, this board finds you guilty of conduct unbecoming of a Mega-City One Judge. Specifically, multiple counts of extortion and theft, and deliberate actions that led to the manslaughter of citizen Virgil Livingstone." Goodman looked around the room. "If any Judge present has anything to say before I pass sentence, speak now."

I glanced toward Gibson again, but he just looked away. *Can't blame him,* I remember thinking. *He's not exactly squeaky-clean himself. But Joe...* That hurt. Joe could have said something. Sure, it mightn't have made the slightest difference, but he could have *tried.* He could have stood up for his brother. Even if he was never going to help me dispose of Livingstone's body and let me go—and I'd been mistaken in thinking he might be flexible enough to see things my way—he could at least have appealed for leniency.

Hell, it wouldn't have surprised me if he'd actually done the opposite and told the Chief Judge to throw the book at me.

With me out of the way, Joe was all set to become top dog in Mega-City One.

And so there was only silence, and my last hope flickered out.

Few of my tutors or mentors were present, and for that I was glad. Judge Morphy, who'd always had the air of a kindly old uncle when he spoke to me and Joe, would have given me *that* look, the look that said, "Rico, you let me down." The same look I'd seen on Kenner's face that time he confronted me about Stacie Quasarano.

Goodman cleared his throat. "Very well. Rico Dredd, you are dishonourably discharged from the Justice Department, and sentenced to a period of no less than twenty years penal servitude."

And that was it. More than a decade as a cadet, a year on the streets, and it was over.

Goodman left the podium and the public gallery was cleared, then six senior Judges marched me toward the side-entrance and into the long corridor that led to the Judge Cubes, where Goodman was already waiting.

To the senior Judges, Goodman said, "Give me a minute with him. Alone."

The Judges hesitated for a moment, then moved away.

Goodman glared at me. "What the hell is *wrong* with you, boy? Top of your class year after year in the academy. Even before you graduated, I had the heads of every department begging me to give you to them." He thumped his fist against his ornate golden chestplate. "You could have been wearing *this* one day. You threw all that away, and for what? For a few handfuls of credits? Grud-damn it, Rico... You know the Law better than anyone!"

For the first time since the investigation began, I spoke. "*Almost* anyone."

"What? What's that supposed to mean? You're talking about Joe? Don't go thinking *he* gets off scot-free. If he'd turned you in earlier, Livingstone would still be alive."

"So now what?" I said. "I spend the next twenty breaking rocks in the Cursed Earth? I can take that. I'll still be younger than you are now when I get out."

"Cursed Earth *nothing*," Goodman snarled at me. "You're going to Titan."

Titan
2080 AD

Seven

When you've lived all your life on Earth suddenly finding yourself on one of Saturn's moons is unbelievably unsettling. The atmosphere on Titan is toxic to humans: mostly nitrogen, with a tiny percentage of methane and hydrogen. And the moon's gravity is only about a seventh of that on Earth, which takes a lot of getting used to.

Most of the time you can't even make out the sun, the atmosphere is so hazy. On the rare occasions when the air is clear and the sky is cloudless, it's just a weak dot in the sky, not much brighter than Venus appears from Earth. And it barely seems to move because—like Earth's moon—Titan's day is the same length as its orbit, which means that one side is always facing Saturn. That's one sunset every sixteen Earth days, just about.

But then there's also a planet-set, when Saturn eclipses the sun. The first time you see that, it's spectacular. It takes hours, of course, with the sunlight rippling through the rings. It's honestly one of the most breathtaking things I have ever seen.

The feeling doesn't last, though. Not when you're working back-breaking twelve-hour shifts out in the low gravity, chained to your fellow inmates, sweating inside your environment suit as you swing a pick-axe over and over at the unyielding ground. Knowing that in all likelihood you're going to die in that Grud-forsaken place, and that meant some other poor drokker would have to spend a day digging your grave.

On my second day on Titan, one of the inmates—a hulking ex-military guy called Cronyn—hit a particularly tough rock and the head came off his pick-axe. It bounced and struck another prisoner right in the environment suit's visor, cracking it.

He was dead in seconds.

The guards' only response was to order Cronyn to pick up the dead man's pick-axe and keep digging.

We worked alongside the corpse for another three hours, until shift's end. Then we carried him between us—still chained—back to the prison.

I WAS SENTENCED in the dying days of December 2080, when Saturn was on the opposite side of the sun to Earth, a distance of one-point-seven billion kilometres. So it wasn't cost-effective to send me to Titan then. I was held in an iso-cube until the following July, when Earth's orbit took it closer to Saturn, only one-point-two billion kilometres.

Even so, the trip took almost two months. Eighty-four prisoners and eight warders trapped in a craft not much bigger than a standard passenger airliner.

To avoid any trouble, we were kept under constant mild sedation. Aware of what was going on around us, and of time passing, but unable to muster the energy to even complain about it. We had been strapped into our seats and hooked up to intravenous lines to keep us alive.

For the most part, the warders stayed in cryogenic suspension. They woke in shifts, two weeks on, three weeks asleep, but there wasn't anything for them to do while they were awake except read or watch movies. That simple privilege was denied to the prisoners. The best we got was every two days being released from our seats—one at a time—and allowed to walk the length of the shuttle a couple of times.

The shuttle touched down on Titan in the late summer of 2081, and the final three days before landing were excruciating. The shuttle had been under constant acceleration since leaving Earth's orbit, and that acceleration provided gravity. But then it had to flip over and use its thrusters to decelerate in order to avoid overshooting its target. For those seventy-two hours, we were subject to five times normal gravity. We could do nothing but sit there and ride out the pain.

One of the prisoners didn't survive that part of the trip. When finally we touched down, the prison's doctor examined him and declared that his heart had failed, probably within the first few minutes.

The rest of us were fitted with electrocuffs, linked together with chains, and led shuffling from the shuttle through a succession of bare, damp, brightly-lit corridors and stairwells into a large glass-domed room, where ten heavily-armed guards were waiting.

One of them stepped forward as we filed into the room, a big man, maybe forty years old. "I am sub-warden Martin Copus. It's my job to keep this operation running smoothly. I take that responsibility very seriously, so you do what you are told and there's a chance that you'll live long enough to see the end of your terms." To the guards, he said, "Line them up. Strip them and scan them. Check their fingerprints, retinas, voice-patterns and DNA against the manifest."

This process took the best part of an hour, but we could deal with that. After the constant five-gees of deceleration, Titan's low gravity was like a long, cool drink on a sweltering summer's day.

Eight of the new arrivals had been smuggling contraband: cash, drugs and electronics that they'd somehow managed to hide from the searches back on Earth. It was confiscated, but none of them were punished.

And then came the needles.

First, they took something away: a litre of blood from every prisoner. "Blood's in short supply around here," Copus told us. "Get into an accident, and you'll be damn grateful we did this." This was followed by a powerful, general-purpose antibiotic, and a number of vaccinations and deep-tissue injections that left us clutching sore, swollen arms and cursing the medics. The last injections before we were issued with the one-size-doesn't-fit-all uniforms was the most painful; a GPS tracker implanted deep into the pelvic girdle. Some of the prisoners had to be held down for that one.

It was only when it was all done that Copus informed us that one of the injections had been a contraceptive. "Lasts about eight months. We don't have a childcare facility here, and we don't intend to start one."

The prisoners' names were read out in alphabetical order, so it wasn't long before they reached me. "Rico Eustace Dredd, former Judge. Mega-City One. Twenty years."

"Take him to the side," Copus said. Two guards grabbed hold of me and dragged me out of the line.

When the roll-call was done, I was one of eleven prisoners who'd been singled out, all Judges.

Copus ordered that the other prisoners be taken to their cells, then he addressed us. "There are rules. Most of them you're gonna find out as and when you need to know. But the chief rule is this: *break* the rules and you will be punished."

He walked right up to me. "You. Name?"

"Rico Dredd." Some of the others had their heads down, but not me. I looked him in the eye. It was the first time anyone had spoken directly to me since we'd left Earth.

"What did they get you on, Rico?"

"They called it corruption."

"It's got to be more than that."

One of the other guards said, "Sir, he killed a civilian. Cleared of murder, but guilty of manslaughter, accepting bribes, subverting the Law for personal gain, possession of illicit substances, abuse of his position—"

"That'll do, Siebert." Copus took a step closer to me, and said, "You look familiar... You're one of Fargo's clones, right? I heard about you. He was a good man. A *great* man. Hard to imagine that his progeny could have sunk so low."

He stepped back and looked around at the rest of the prisoners. "The minimum sentence on Titan is twenty years. You know why that is? Because that's how long you have to work here to justify the cost of the trip. This is a mining colony, just like the old one on Enceladus before that moon became too unstable to mine the iridium. The work here is hard, and dangerous, and for that they want people like you. Tough guys." He said that last part with a snort. "All of you have been deemed too dangerous to imprison on Earth or even the Lunar colonies. Titan is about as far away as you can be sent while still being cost-effective."

Copus began to pace back and forth, staring at each of us as he passed, and I figured he was memorising our faces. "And you used to be *Judges*. Five from Mega-City One. Three from Texas City. One each from Mega-City Two, Brit-Cit and East-Meg One. You were raised in the toughest academies on Earth, so that means you think you understand how hard life can be. Well, you're going to learn exactly how wrong that is. I guarantee that by the end of your first week, you'll be wishing you'd been executed instead."

He turned to me again. "You. Rico... They must really be scared of you, huh? Fargo's little boy turned bad. I can see that. And you've got that 'I can take it' look in your eyes." He smiled at that. "You'll learn, boy."

I said, "Don't call me 'boy.'"

I steeled myself for a beating, but it didn't happen. Instead, Copus's smile grew even wider. "I'll call you whatever the hell I like. You're not in charge any more. All of you are gonna have to understand that. You've got no power here. None. You have fewer rights on Titan than even the lowest citizens in your cities."

Copus turned to the prisoner next to me. "You. The sov. Sentence?"

The other guard, Siebert, said, "She doesn't speak English, sir. Zera Kurya. Thirty years for killing four other Judges. The exact circumstances aren't clear, but apparently she's never denied the charges."

Copus moved on down the line, checking us out one by one, and then returned to the centre of the room. "All right. Your first shift starts in a little under four hours. Shifts are twelve hours on, eight hours off. You get one day of rest for every eighteen days worked, and that's the only vacation you'll have. You get sick enough that you can't work, those days don't count toward your time here. So if your sentence is twenty years, then by Grud you'll *work* those twenty years. And speaking of that... Today is Day One. The time you spent waiting for the shuttle to leave Earth, and the sixty-two days you've just spent in space, do *not* count toward your sentence."

He gave us a few seconds to let that sink in, then said, "Insubordination will result in days added to your sentence. Harm a fellow prisoner to a degree that he or she can't work, days added. Each escape attempt will result in *months* added. Not that there's any *point* in trying to escape: we're alone on Titan and there's no way off this rock without a ship, and even if you somehow managed to steal one, there's nowhere to go. Head for Earth and you'd be shot down before you reached the asteroid belt. So you're here, and you work. Simple as that."

I asked, "The rest of the prisoners get the same lecture?" Then, quickly, I added, "I'm not being insubordinate, boss. I'm just curious."

Copus walked slowly toward me. "The other new inmates, Rico, are civilians. I know that Mega-City One rarely sends civilians here, but the other cities do. The civilians get a different lecture. But you lot are special. You were Judges. You all think you'll be able to ride this out, to coast your way through. Trust me, it won't be like that. I hate bent Judges, Rico, so I'm gonna bend you 'til you *break*."

I smiled. "That sounds like a challenge." Again, I braced myself for a beating, but again it didn't come.

Copus turned to Siebert. "Chain them, take them to their cells. And prep them for the first shift."

The guards chained our cuffs together, and as we were being filed out of the room, Copus called out, "Rico? That smart-mouth attitude? You'll want to drop that. It'll do you no favours here. The only way off this rock for you people is to keep your heads down, work hard and pray to whatever god you believe in that you can make it through. *I'm* the law here. Remember that. You push me too hard, and you'll get the treatment."

He didn't say what "the treatment" was, and we didn't ask, but he clearly meant it to sound unsettling.

We found out a few hours later. Some of the other prisoners—hardened men and women who could crack open a human skull and eat its contents with a spoon and not think twice about it—broke down when they realised what it meant.

Eight

"INSIDE," SIEBERT SAID, gesturing to what was to be my home for the next two decades. It was barred on three sides—there were occupied cells on either side of mine—with a solid stone wall at the back.

I was last in our group to be assigned a cell, so I knew what to expect: "Walk to the wall. Stand facing it with your feet apart. Rest your forehead on the wall."

I did as instructed, and Siebert unlocked my cuffs. "Next meal's in two hours, inmate. Twenty minutes allocated. Then you'll be fitted for your environment suit." He'd said the same thing to every prisoner, in the same bored tone.

Siebert was tall and wiry, a mean-looking drokker who was smart enough to never find himself alone with a prisoner. This wasn't like a prison movie, where there's always one guard who's unbelievably sadistic, who punishes the inmates to the point where they snap. Siebert was tough, unpleasant, but he had a full understanding of who he was dealing with.

The meal was simple; a scratched plastic bowl containing some kind of bland oatmeal-like paste, a cup of warm water that had a mild metallic tang, and a handful of raw carrots that were so pale they could have been parsnips.

Some of the other new prisoners weren't able to keep it down, they had been so long without solid food. Me, I got cramps and a bad case of the sweats after only a few mouthfuls. Another prisoner, a lank-haired, hawk-faced man in his thirties, was hovering around our table, constantly asking, "You gonna finish that, fish? You eatin' that? Lemme lick the bowl, huh?"

He tried it on me. "Hey, fishy-fish. You gimme the rest of your dinner an' I'll make it worth your while."

"Take a hike, creep," I told him.

"*Not* a creep," he said. "*Not* a creep, new fish." He stared at me with wide, twitching eyes that didn't seem to be able to blink in unison. "You're goin' out today, first time steppin' out into the Bronze, right?" Then he paused. "Damn, I probably sound like a crazy person. The Bronze is what we call the outside, because it's all brown and stuff. Guy who came here from Enceladus fancied himself as a poet, he called it that. My name's Pea. Yours?"

"Rico." I decided to give the scuzzball a break. I'd learned on the streets of Mega-City One that crazy people could be very useful. Everyone underestimates them, and their behaviour can cover up a lot of actions that might otherwise draw suspicion. In a place like this, it might help to know someone who could get around without being noticed.

"You here for the twenty, Rico-fish, or did you earn more than that?" Pea asked.

"Twenty," I told him. I figured that was his way of judging how dangerous someone was. "What about you?"

"Thirty-five. I'll be seventy when my time is up, if I make it." He grinned, showing off his meagre collection of brown teeth. "You were a Judge, weren't you? Word gets around. Me, I got railroaded. I'm innocent."

"Sure you are."

"No, seriously. Totally innocent. I was a quality controller at Resyk in Meg Two. There was an accident, people died, I got the blame."

"I remember that," I said. "It made the news in Mega-City One. You were supposed to be monitoring the fluid filters but instead you were pilfering the corpses for gold fillings and pace-makers to sell on the black market. A valve failed and thousands of litres of body fluids bypassed the filters and ended up in your sector's drinking water. Seventy thousand citizens poisoned by the faecal matter of four hundred corpses. Twelve deaths."

Pea nodded. "That's the story they reported. The truth is, I was off-shift when it happened but the Resyk controller had been angling to replace me with a droid, and this was the perfect chance to get rid of me." He reached out his hand. "Elemeno Jameson Pea."

I shook his hand, but I still didn't believe his declaration of innocence. "Elemeno Pea. Parents had a sense of humour?"

"Yeah. Still, coulda been worse. My old man wanted to call me Asparagus." He shrugged. "You want my advice, Rico? You hafta be like a raft on the ocean, got that? Don't make waves...." Pea put out his hand, palm-down, then slowly and smoothly moved it away. "Just go with the flow. You might make it. You might. You don't wanna end up a mod, like *this* poor drokker." He pointed toward the door, where a figure was entering.

The man was tall, with a strong build. He was shirtless, and it looked like his skin was covered in grey dust. Later, I found out that *was* his skin.

Outside, in Titan's dense atmosphere, a human cannot survive without an environment suit. It's cold—eighty below, on a good day—and the air is toxic. But there were certain parts of the mines where an environment suit isn't practical. Many of the tunnels have narrow passages where a suit will snag, and on the open plains during a dust-storm a suit'll be shredded to rags in minutes.

So some prisoners are modified. Their skin is injected with an almost indestructible polymer. Their eyes are coated with a thinner, transparent layer of the same thing. Their lungs are replaced with a biomechanical breathing apparatus that converts the methane to oxygen. Their noses are removed, replaced with dust-filters, and their mouths sealed. For as long as the prisoner is on Titan, he or she won't be able eat or drink or even breathe normally.

This is "the treatment." Those who've been subject to it are called "mods" by the other prisoners.

My new friend Elemeno Pea said, "They say it hurts like Hades on a hotplate getting it done, hurts ten times more getting it reversed. But it allows you to work in the Bronze without a suit, and Copus likes that. Makes him less inclined to add days. Plus these mods don't do twelve hours on and eight hours off like us. They do ten-on and ten-off. Has to be that way, because they hafta purge their nose-filters every ten hours. That's something you don't wanna see if you've just eaten." He slapped me on the shoulder. "What do you say, Rico-fish? Sound tempting?"

"Not especially."

"Doesn't matter none if it *is* tempting, anyway, because it's not up to us to decide if we want it done. That's up to the sub-warden. You get on his wrong side, an' he will literally tear your lungs out. And I literally *do* mean literally."

THE REASON THE prison existed really was simple economics: the surface of Titan was rich in iridium deposits. Donny Guildford, a prisoner from Brit-Cit in the cell to the left of mine, told me about it.

"Iridium is the most corrosion-resistant element known. Very useful stuff, when alloyed with platinum or osmium or titanium. It's really hard to find on Earth, but it's common in meteorites and here in the outer system."

Donny Guildford had been a civilian, a research scientist who'd taken to settling inter-departmental disputes with tiny amounts of thallium. He was quite an expert with poisons and, according to his prosecutors, had more than ten kills under his belt.

Guildford was also a mod. He'd been caught attempting to strangle another inmate to death—self-defence, he claimed—and sub-warden Copus had ordered that he be given the treatment.

"The operation takes five days, Rico," Guildford told me late one night. "Heard they've got new drugs now that can make you forget the pain, but not when they did it to me. Five days of the purest hell you can imagine."

Guildford was sitting on the floor, resting against the bars that separated his cell from mine.

"They strap you down first. Arms, legs, head. Make sure you can't move. The eyes are the worst. Some guys say that the lungs hurt more, but not me. They hit you with a paralysing agent so you can't squirm away, then they use a suction device to pop out your eyes. Spray them with the polymer. And even if they do now have something to make you forget the operation, it still hurts like drokk for months afterwards. Every breath, every blink... You won't *believe* the pain, man. Just pray that they don't do it to you."

He twisted around and looked at me. It was hard to look back, but I wasn't going to let myself flinch. He tapped the voicebox fitted to his throat. "Wasn't for this, I wouldn't even be able to speak."

"Your mouth's been sealed—how do you eat?" I asked.

Guildford took hold of the voicebox and pulled. It came away from his neck with a wet sound. He handed it to me, but I didn't want to touch it. It was covered in saliva and mucus. Guildford reconnected the voicebox and said, "They give us a paste, like baby-food. Have to push it in with my fingers. It's drokkin' *disgusting*, man." He shrugged. "But I suppose it does have its advantages. Out in the Bronze, before they did this to me, I was constantly watching the oxygen pressure on my suit. Don't need to worry about that now."

EVERY PRISON HAS its own hierarchy among the inmates. It didn't matter how tough you'd been on the outside, when you arrived in the prison you were a new fish, on the bottom rung of the ladder, and the older fish did anything and everything to make sure you stayed there.

I quickly learned that many of the established prisoners particularly despised former Judges. Donny Guildford had warned me to watch my back, but I hadn't paid him any attention. I was a Judge. I'd excelled in the toughest environment on Earth. I could take anything they decided to throw at me.

My first encounter with Register Forbes came a week after I arrived. Forbes was fifty years old, slightly balding, a once-solid build now heavy with age and lethargy. He had a lot of connections and he knew how to acquire things for other inmates. That made him powerful, and powerful men get to thinking they're untouchable and immortal.

I didn't know who Forbes was when he shoulder-bumped me as I passed him in the corridor, but I knew enough to tell that it was a test.

I called him on it. "Watch where you're going, stomm-sucker."

And instantly I was surrounded by five very large, dangerous-looking inmates, all scars, tattoos and knuckles.

One of them pushed his head so close to mine that when he spoke, tiny specks of spittle landed on my face. "*You* watch who you're talking to, fish! Mister Forbes doesn't get out of your way. *You* get out of *his*."

I said, "If Mister Forbes has a problem with me, Mister Forbes can grow a pair and tell me himself."

The bruiser telegraphed the punch. I dodged it easily, but didn't strike back: I was testing them, too. I'd figured it wouldn't be long before something like this happened.

The bruiser took another swing—I swear his fist was almost as big as my head—and again I dodged it. And then two of his friends grabbed hold of my arms.

They knew I was a Judge. How could they have *not* known? Sub-warden Copus had effectively tagged all the Judges the day we arrived by separating us from the other prisoners. So if Forbes knew I was a Judge, he must have known what was coming next.

It was over in seconds. I kicked the bruiser in the groin, he doubled over and—using his friends' grips on my arms as leverage—I jerked both my feet up and slammed them hard into his head. Hard enough to send him sprawling and force the others to loosen their hold. I fell back between them, rolled onto my feet and crouched.

The two who'd grabbed me started to move toward me again, but Forbes called them off. "Let him be."

He came closer, looked down at me. "You're fast. I've heard about you, Rico Dredd. They say you were one of the best, until you turned bad."

"They're wrong on both counts," I said. "I never turned bad. I just had my own way of doing things that didn't sit well with the rest of the Justice Department. And I was not *one* of the best." I straightened up. "I was *the* best."

"They caught you. Can't have been *that* good."

"There were extenuating circumstances. What do you want, Forbes?"

For a moment he peered at me as though he was asking himself that same question, then he said, "I'm always on the lookout for people who might be useful to me, and I've a feeling you could be very useful indeed." He extended his hand. "I think you and I will be strong allies."

I ignored the hand. "That's not your decision. What are you in for?"

"Murder. Multiple counts."

I didn't ask him if he was guilty. I could see it in his face. "I don't ally myself with scum."

Still with the same calm, detached manner, Forbes said, "Then you're going to be lonely in this place. Listen to me, Rico. I can smooth the path for you. Make things easier."

"Things are not supposed to be easy, creep," I said. "This is a prison, not a day-centre. The Law put us here to punish us. We do our time, and we do *not* coast on the backs of others."

Again, he regarded me silently for a few seconds. "You're not a Judge any more. You're one of us. Here, you play by our rules. Or you don't get to play at all. See, there are *degrees* of punishment. Some prisoners—the weak—have no choice but to lie down and let the strong walk all over them. But some of us, by our very nature, will always rise to the top of any given situation. You strike me as a survivor, Rico. You should—"

By then, I had turned around and was walking away.

Forbes called after me. "You're making a mistake. This offer only comes once. If you're not with me, then you don't get my protection. You know what that means in this place? It means you're a *dead man walking* unless you get back here and *pay attention when I'm talking to you!*" He had to shout that last part.

In the cells that night, Guildford told me that I had written my own obituary. "He's gonna come for you. Well, not him, but one of his guys."

"Let them come," I said. "I can take them."

"No, Rico, you don't get it. Forbes knows this place inside-out and upside-down. He knows all the guards, and he's friends with most of them. That's how he gets stuff in. It's why he's *protected.* He used to *be* a guard, back in the old prison on Enceladus. That's where he got his nickname; he pretty much ran the prison, got all the day-to-day stuff done. The warden would say, 'I need ten prisoners to swamp out the lower cells' and Register would schedule it and pick the prisoners *and* the guards. He gave all the easy duties to his friends, dumped the crap on anyone who complained or criticised him."

"He was the power behind the throne?"

"And then some. When they were preparing to evacuate Enceladus he was in charge of the flight manifests and the supplies and everything. A couple of the other guards caught him short-loading the iridium shipments back to Earth, and they threatened to squeal on him if he didn't cut them in. He made like he was going to do it, but on the next shift he sent them out into the Bronze with sabotaged oxygen tanks. They were rigged to read like they were full, but they only had a couple of minutes of air."

I nodded slowly. "He was caught, arrested, and ended up back here."

"No. They didn't even send him home first. The warden's a Judge; he sentenced Register on the spot. One day Register's got a cushy room in the guards' quarters, next day he's in a cell. But the thing is, he didn't rat out anyone else he was working with. So the next day after *that*, Register is moved to a *better* cell, and his pals let the other prisoners know that he's protected. Anything happens to him, they'll get the treatment."

I said, "I thought that Copus was the one who decided who got the treatment?"

"Officially Copus and the warden both have to agree to it, but the warden doesn't care and Copus listens to Siebert. And Siebert is one of Register's friends."

With this new knowledge, the next day I made peace, of a sort, with Register Forbes. I found one of his thugs—the bruiser, now sporting an ancient, grubby neck-brace—and told him I wanted to meet.

I was brought to Register's cell. Compared with the rest of us, he lived in a palace. It was twice the size of the other cells, and featured four stone walls—not a bar in sight. There was a toilet with an actual seat, and more than one blanket on the bed. Not that he'd need them; his stone-walled cell was considerably less draughty than any other place I'd seen in the prison.

Register was lying on the bed, and when he saw me enter he tossed his book aside and stood up. "So you changed your mind, Rico? Someone's been talking to you, is my guess. Someone who knows the score."

"You have friends back on Earth," I said.

"This much is true."

"So do I. And *my* friends are Judges. You think you can make things tough for me here? That's a hangnail compared to what my friends can do to yours. To your family."

"Huh," he said. "That a *threat*?"

"Yes. And if you want clarification, try this: you hurt me, and every one of your friends back home will lose their eyes."

I stepped closer to him, and his bodyguards rushed at me from the doorway. I elbowed one in the face, hard. I grabbed the wrist of another with both hands, then jerked him toward me and kicked him deep in the armpit. I let his dislocated arm drop as he screamed, then rounded on the third guard—a woman I hadn't seen before. She was a lot shorter than me, but that didn't stop me launching a right jab at her throat.

She expertly blocked it, then swung at me. I dropped into a crouch and kicked out at her knees. She side-stepped the kick, but her movement took her away from me long enough for me to get back on my feet.

There was a flurry of vicious punches, jabs and kicks on both sides, all of which were dodged or blocked.

It only came to an end when two of Register's other guards jumped me from behind. They dragged me away from the woman and held me tight while Register checked her over.

"You're not hurt?" he asked. He sounded genuinely concerned.

She shook her head as she continued to glare at me. "Nothing that won't heal. Drokker's stronger than me. Faster too. He's a keeper."

Register glanced at me. "I don't know... He's dangerous. And he can't be trusted."

"We'll need him." She pulled herself away from Register, and approached me. "Where'd you serve?"

"Mega-City One. You?"

"Same. Four years in Meg-South." The woman was in her

mid-twenties, and very definitely had the look of a former Judge; determined, confident, capable. She wasn't what you'd call attractive—certainly not my type—but there was something about her that piqued my interest.

"What did they get you on?" I asked.

"Riot control. I opened fire on the crowd. Turned out there was a couple of undercover Judges among them. One of them survived, testified against me." Without blinking or looking away, she continued, "Seems the Department has a problem with Judges walking up to fourteen wounded, unconscious rioters and putting bullets in their brains. What about you?"

"Corruption, they called it. And there was a death. Accidental, but... a fellow Judge didn't see it that way."

She tilted her head a little to the side as she gazed at me. "Has to be more to it than that."

"There is." I offered her my hand. "Rico Dredd."

She shook it. "Adelaide Montenegro." Her hand was warm, and she held onto mine for a second longer than necessary.

To the side, Register Forbes said, "If you two are done sizing each other up? Rico, we were in the middle of threatening each other. Where do we stand on that?"

I said to him, "Forbes, I don't want to be part of your crew. You stay the drokk away from me, I leave you and your friends with all limbs and digits intact. How does that sound?" I turned and walked toward the door.

"You'll be back, Rico!" he called after me. "Sooner or later, you'll *need* me for something. You'll come back. And when you do, if you don't want to end up like your friend Donny Guildford, you'll come back on your *knees*!"

Nine

I WAS ALMOST eight months into my sentence on Titan when I first realised that escape might be possible.

The other prisoners talked about escape all the time, of course, but most of them didn't have the understanding to grasp just how unlikely it was. They'd talk about using the mining tools as weapons to hold the guards hostage, or hiding out in one of the exhausted mine-shafts.

Elemeno Pea was particularly excitable when it came to escape plans, and he had a hundred of them, not one of which was remotely practical. "We hide all the iridium we find," was one such plan. "We dump it deep inside one of the exhausted mine shafts. Then when the bosses see that there's no more iridium, they'll have to abandon the prison 'cause it'll not be, whaddayacall, cost-effective any more. That means sending us back to Earth. From there, we can get away easy."

Another of his great plans was that we'd kill a random prisoner every day, but make it look like suicide: "They won't keep us here if they think we're all gonna top ourselves!"

And then there was Pea's masterpiece of lateral stupidity, which he explained to me and Guildford one day as we were picking fruit in the prison's huge hydroponic gardens: "Gravity's so low on Titan, escape velocity is *way* down. So, see, what we need is to build a giant sling-shot. One of those tree-bucket things."

"A trebuchet?" I asked.

"Yeah, if you want to get all fancy about it. So we build one of them and fling ourselves out of the atmosphere."

Guildford said, "Where we'll die in space."

"Yes. No! See, we make the tray-bushy thing big enough that it can fling a cargo container. We'll be inside it, with supplies and so on. And we'll seal it up first, make sure it's airtight."

"And *then* what, Pea?" I asked. The man was peering over the edge of insanity at the best of times, but he was just about the only entertainment we had. "We'd need some form of propulsion or we'd just get pulled back to Titan. Or get caught in Saturn's gravity well."

"Hey, I thought of that too. We take along a whole bunch of other prisoners, then, when we're in space, we throw them out one at a time. It's Newton's Third Law of Motion, right? Every action has an equal and opposite *re*action. We throw out a guy, and he goes one way while we go the opposite way."

"And after the first guy we throw out, why would the others allow us to throw *them* out?" I asked.

"Well, they'll be dead. We'll kill them first. Dead bodies are lighter than live ones, which'll make it easier for the tray-bushay to get the cargo container into space."

Guildford said, "Dead bodies *aren't* lighter, Pea. Someone who worked in Resyk ought to know that. They..." He stopped himself. "Why am I even *arguing* this with you? We can't build a trebuchet because it would take years and the guards would *see* it!"

"Not to mention that it wouldn't work," I said. "Besides, it's asking a lot that we put our faith in someone who pronounces the word 'escape' with an X."

A guard yelled over at us: "Shut up and get back to work!"

We'd been on garden duty for a week already, working in the vast dome, picking the fruits and vegetables that grew to enormous size in the low gravity. Some prisoners believed that it was preferable to working in the mine-shafts, but not me. It was tough, endless, back-breaking work, and we sweltered under the powerful lamps and choked on the rich, cloying scents of the flowering trees. So much greenness made me uncomfortable: I was raised in a concrete-and-steel city where ninety per cent of the population had never seen a real tree.

There were fewer guards than in the rest of the compound since we didn't have power-tools, but they kept a close watch on us nonetheless, in case we ate as we picked.

When the shift was done, we were frisked, then chained once more and led back to our cells.

As we reached the exit and the guards fumbled with the ancient locks on the huge gates, I looked back over the gardens. It was an impressive sight: a dozen square kilometres of fields of wheat and corn, orchards and vegetable patches and herb gardens. The plants provided the prison with oxygen as well as food. Without them, the prison would not be viable.

And an important thought began to form...

I did some quick mental calculations, but the answer didn't seem right, so I started over. Again, the same answer.

By the time I reached my cell, I realised that I had stumbled upon something that I was sure none of the other prisoners had discovered.

There *was* a way off Titan. It wouldn't be easy, but it could be done.

I WAS OUT in the Bronze when the storm hit us. We were a chain-gang of twenty inmates and five guards working on a newly-discovered deposit about three hundred kilometres east of the prison.

We'd been there for three days already, spending our off-time in the huge, low-slung, wide-wheeled transport vehicle that the guards jokingly referred to as the School Bus, and were scheduled to stay out there for another week.

The new iridium deposit was the debris from a large meteorite strike a few thousand years ago. Our job was to scan the surface for fragments—in Titan's low gravity, even a low-velocity impact could spread the fragments up to a kilometre away—then dig them out of the surrounding dirt. Any fragments too large to lift were flagged for later retrieval by a powered digger. We loaded the smaller fragments into two-wheeled barrows, pushed them over the rough ground to the massive trailer attached to the back of the bus. It was exhausting and mind-numbingly tedious, but then I'd yet to discover a job in the prison that was anything but.

Siebert was overseeing the dig, which meant that he'd had his pick of the prisoners. Since it meant time away from the prison compound, there'd been a lot of volunteers. Siebert picked Register Forbes and his crew, and Register had told him to pick me, Guildford and Pea.

In the months since our encounter, Register had made it clear that he wanted me working for him. He could have strong-armed me, or threatened my friends, but he was smarter than that. About once a week he or Montenegro would call on me and ask, "Changed your mind yet?" My answer was always in the negative, but that didn't stop them.

So twenty inmates and five guards piled into the back of the School Bus and set off on the last journey that most of us would ever make. But of course we didn't know that.

The storm hit hard, and fast. The sensors on the bus were barely adequate; we had less than a minute's warning.

Siebert's voice came blaring over our helmet-radios: "Get back to the bus! Now! Storm coming—a bad one!"

On Titan, the weather comes at you like an invisible psychopath wielding an irresistible grudge and a stealth chainsaw. One minute it's all calm and clear skies—well, as clear as they ever get, which isn't saying much—and the next, there's two-hundred-KPH winds and hailstones the size of your fist. I've heard that it wasn't always so extreme, but a few years back some of the bigger cities collaborated in an attempt to terraform Titan, to turn it into another Earth. They installed atmosphere processors and weather-controlling satellites, and attempted to cap a couple of active volcanoes. They didn't want the same thing happening on Titan that had destroyed the mine on Enceladus.

It failed quite spectacularly when one of the volcanoes erupted prematurely and incinerated eighty-one engineers and a billion credits' worth of equipment. The project was abandoned, leaving only the engineers' mining base and a handful of outstations. But the volcanic eruption had released millions of tonnes of iridium ore... No one wanted to leave that behind, but no one was dumb enough to volunteer to stay and mine it. The best compromise was to give the hard work to those members of society whose lives weren't worth much.

The prisoners were always chained around the waist. The chains were hardened steel, tough enough that it would take several hours to cut through with the tools we were given. I was chained to Guildford, Pea and a guy I didn't know. We'd been maybe two hundred metres from the bus, returning with barrow-loads of iridium ore, when we got the call. We made it back seconds before the first hailstones slammed into the side of the bus.

The bus's windows were made of thick plastiglass. Tough enough to withstand the storm, clear enough that we could see the others caught outside, abandoning their barrows and pick-axes and running hell-for-leather for safety.

Guildford was next to me at the window, looking out. A hailstone exploded against the glass right in front of us. "Jovus... This is gonna be a bad one!"

To the east, the sky was darkening.

Ten

OUTSIDE, A HAILSTONE struck one of Forbes's men in the back of the head. He went down at once, and never moved again. Or not voluntarily: his colleagues were still chained to him.

As they tried to drag the corpse over the hail-scattered ground, one of them was hit in the elbow. Though it should have been impossible over the roar of the storm, I swear I heard the crack.

"Get out there!" I shouted to Siebert. "Unlock them!"

He shook his head. "There's no point. It'd take too long for me to put on my suit."

"Then give *me* the key. I'll do it!"

He looked at me like I was crazy. "No drokkin' way are you getting my key!"

Another flurry of hailstones ripped into the side of the bus, hard enough to rock it, and outside I saw the dead man's colleagues drop. The last one alive was smart: with considerable effort he pulled his friends' corpses over himself.

All we could do was wait. All five guards—unencumbered by chains—were back in the bus, but of the twenty prisoners, only eight of us had made it.

Someone said, "Food and water'll last longer this way, I guess."

I turned from the window to see who'd spoken, and saw Register Forbes slam his fist into the side of another prisoner's head. "Those are my people out there!"

Again, I said to Siebert, "Give me the key."

He backed away from me. "No. It's policy. No matter what happens, I can't give a key to a prisoner."

"I'm not going to *report* you, damn it! That guy's still *alive* out there—better to go back with nine prisoners than eight! Just give me the drokkin' *key!*"

Forbes said, "Do it, Siebert. Where's he going to run to?"

Siebert wouldn't look me in the eye as he unclipped the electronic key from his belt.

Guildford said to me, "Let me do it. I don't need a suit."

"I'm faster than you, and smaller," I said. "Less of a target. Siebert?"

Siebert placed his thumb on the key's scanpad. "You've got a hundred seconds before—"

"I know," I told him as I grabbed the key from his hand and ran for the airlock. After one hundred seconds the key would become inert again. It was a security measure, in case a prisoner ever managed to snatch a key from a guard. "Keep the airlock open!"

Outside, the wind threatened to lift me off my feet as I half-ran, half-crawled toward the downed prisoner. I tried shouting, letting the fallen man know that help was coming, but my voice was swamped in the roar of the storm.

The ground was treacherous, slick with fragmented hailstones as a fresh flurry pounded down around me, ripping chunks out of the dirt.

As I reached the bodies, a hailstone the size of a football missed my head by centimetres. Later, Pea told me that they had watched it strike the ground behind me and bounce clear over the bus.

I saw a gloved hand protruding from beneath the bodies, and grabbed it. It grabbed back—he was still alive.

I took hold of the topmost body—it was a prisoner I'd seen working in the gardens—and dragged it clear, then lost a few seconds trying to get the key to work.

It was only when I was hauling the man free that I realised it wasn't a man at all, but Adelaide Montenegro, my fellow former Judge.

She nodded at me as I helped her to her feet, then she began to scramble over the growing piles of hailstones toward the bus.

I followed her, aware that at any moment we could be struck from behind.

By the time we reached the bus, the hail was already up to the airlock's outer door. Forbes was inside, kicking out the hail almost as fast as it was piling up.

Montenegro lunged for the airlock, and Forbes grabbed her hand, helped her the rest of the way. Then he reached out for me.

I almost hesitated. I didn't want someone like Forbes to have any reason to think I owed him, even in a situation like this.

But then, I *had* just saved his colleague's life.

I grabbed his arm and allowed him to help me into the airlock.

He slammed the outer doors closed, and the roar from outside subsided a little.

As we left the airlock, Siebert was waiting for us. "I've heard of storms like this lasting hours. Then we're looking at digging the damn bus out."

Forbes said, "Well, now, thanks to Rico, we have one more person to dig."

"Right," Siebert said. He held out his hand, palm up. "Key?"

I pointed outside. "I had more important things on my mind than your stupid key. You want it, go out and fetch it for yourself."

Naturally, Siebert ordered the other guards to search me, but it wasn't hard to hide the key in the folds of my environment suit when I removed it.

The storm lasted for nine hours, a relentless, deafening assault that shook the bus with every impact and more than once threatened to shatter a window.

I eventually fell into an uneasy sleep and woke to a darkened bus, thinking that night had come; but no, this was Titan. Night was another six days away. We were just buried under countless tonnes of hail.

Siebert and another of the guards—a thin, stoic man called Vickers—were awake, sitting in the cab. When Siebert saw me move, he beckoned me closer.

In a low voice, he said, "Rico... The engine's dead. Don't know whether it's just a loose connection or something more serious, but"—he tapped the dashboard readouts—"there's nothing happening here. Radio's shot, too. Copus knows where we are, but we don't know how badly *they* were hit by the storm. It could be some time before we're rescued."

"So we rescue ourselves," I said. "Dig our way out."

"And go where?" Vickers asked. "We're hundreds of kilometres from the prison and we're the only people on the whole damn planet."

Siebert said, "It's a moon, not a planet."

"Like *that* makes a drokkin' difference."

"We're not alone," I said. "But right now, getting out of here is our first priority. Even if Copus sends people after us, we don't know how deep we're buried. From the air, they might not spot us. We might never be found." I tilted my head back, looked up at the roof. "How thick is the armour plating on this thing?"

"Three centimetres, maybe four," Siebert said. "We don't have anything that can cut through it. And we can't go out through the airlock. There's a wall of ice out there, and all the digging tools are outside. I say we sit tight."

Vickers nodded. "Food'll last us a couple of weeks. Three if we're careful. Same with the air, plus there's oxygen in the suits. And if we want water, we have all the ice we'll ever need outside."

"The ice isn't *water*, it's frozen methane," said Guildford, coming up behind me. "Though it might come in useful if there's no sign of rescue and we're slowly starving to death. We could thaw some out and gas ourselves instead."

"Methane gas is flammable in oxygen," I said, thinking aloud.

Siebert said, "You think we could burn our way out?"

I started to say that it might work, but Guildford interrupted me. "Unlikely. If the mix of oxygen to methane is too thick or too thin, it won't burn. A bigger problem is that if the ice *is* methane, it won't be around long. It's got a much lower melting-point than frozen water. That's not as good as it sounds: if it melts too quickly there's a possibility we could drown. I doubt this bus was built to float."

THE BUS'S BACK-UP power failed on the evening of the second day. That is, the second Earth day.

Most of us were awake when the interior lights dimmed and faded. The darkness wasn't complete—it was still daytime on Titan, and enough light filtered through the hail outside that we could still just about see.

"Damn, it's *quiet* out there," Vickers said.

He was right. There was the constant dripping of melting methane-ice, but that only served to heighten the silence. There was no wind, no engine-hum of an approaching rescue craft... And something else was missing. It took me a moment to realise what it was. "It's quiet in here, too. The air-recycler must be on the same circuits as the lights."

Pea jumped to his feet. "Drokk! How long is the air in here going to last?"

"Don't worry about that," Donny Guildford said. "You'll freeze to death before you suffocate."

Siebert said, "Everyone, suit-up. And if any of you have any ideas how we can get out of here, now's the time to let the rest of us know."

Guildford said, "Bet you all wish you'd had the treatment now, right?"

"Yeah, that doesn't help," I told him, pulling on my environment suit. "The first thing we need to establish is how deep we're buried. I say we have no option but to start digging. We open the outer airlock door and see what happens. If the hail spills in, then it's not all frozen into one mass. That means we'll have a chance of getting out."

Siebert nodded. "All right. But we're only sending out *one* person. And that's Montenegro."

The former Judge looked up at him. "Me? No way."

"You're the smallest. That means you won't have to dig so much."

Guildford said, "It's not about size, Siebert. It's about *strength*. And one isn't enough. Me and Rico will do it."

There were no objections, not even when I took the oxygen tank from one of the spare suits.

Without power, we had to open the airlock doors manually, which took some effort. The guards closed and sealed the inner airlock door behind us, then Guildford and I stood facing the outer door.

"Ready for this?" he asked.

"Don't have a lot of other options."

We grabbed hold of the lever next to the door, and pulled. I had to brace my feet against the wall, but we managed it. The methane ice on the outer door cracked as the door swung in, revealing a densely-packed wall of apple-sized hailstones. They didn't fall.

"That's not good," Guildford said. He reached out and poked at the wall with his fingertips, hesitated a second, then pressed harder. "Seems solid... although it's melting."

Together, we tried pushing at the wall, then kicking at it. Too solid to move, and too slick to hold onto.

Guildford said, "Rico, we could be looking at two or three metres. Maybe more. Nothing short of a concussion grenade is going to get us through this. We're going to have to wait until it melts further."

"That might not be as long as you think," I said. "Look down."

He looked. At our feet was a pool of liquid methane about a centimetre deep, and growing. "Damn. That a good sign or a bad one?"

"Wish I knew. Could be that it's melting from the ground up rather than from the top. If that's the case, then—" We felt the bus shift, very slightly, to the left.

Guildford said, "Okay... That's definitely *not* a good sign."

The bus lurched again, more noticeably.

"I know we're not parked on a *hill*," he said. "So what in Grud's name is happening out there?"

We never found out exactly what happened. The best guess is that the bus was frozen into the ice, and the ice was melting under it.

The bus rocked and swayed for another four hours. At times, we had no doubt that we were moving, that the whole ice floe was sliding, dragging the bus with it.

Many of the more serious lurches—the ones that had us clutching at walls and seat-backs for support—were accompanied by deafening cracks from outside.

The walls trembled as the bus's wheels were dragged over the ground, and there was nothing we could do but wait it out.

The air inside the bus grew stale, our breath misting as the temperature dropped. Frost formed on the inside of the windows, and we were forced to seal our helmets and pray that the oxygen lasted long enough for us to be rescued.

Except for Guildford, of course.

I saw Vickers and Siebert at the bus's controls. They had the dashboard panels removed, and had been poring over the wiring for hours, to no great effect.

I sat with Pea and Montenegro and Forbes and Guildford, and countless ideas were raised, discussed and dismissed. Except for Pea's ideas, which were dismissed without discussion to save time.

And gradually I became aware that Vickers kept looking in our direction, and of the air of conspiracy about him and Siebert. You quickly develop a feel for that sort of thing when you're a Judge.

Montenegro seemed to be aware of it too; she moved closer to me and said, "Something's wrong."

"I know," I told her, keeping my voice low. "We should have been found by now, no matter how far the ice has carried us. I think we need some answers." I stood up, stepped over sleeping bodies on my way to the cab.

"That's close enough, Rico," Siebert said, his hand drifting toward his gun. "What do you want?"

"Why haven't they come for us?"

Vickers said, "We talked about that. The bus's controls are shot; they can't lock—"

"Drokk the controls," I said. "Every prisoner on this bus has a GPS tracking implant. You know that."

The two men briefly exchanged a glance, and my suspicions were confirmed. There was no GPS implant. It was just another ruse to keep the prisoners in line.

And I was sure that even if we *were* rescued, sub-warden Copus would have us killed before we could let the other prisoners know that the GPS wasn't real. I gave them a way out. "It doesn't work this far from the prison, does it?"

"Radius of about ninety kilometres," Vickers said. Lying.

Siebert added, "And if you even *think* of mentioning that to the others, I'll happily put a bullet in your brain."

"What would be the point of telling them?" I asked. "If someone escapes from the prison there's nowhere to *go*. Look, we want to get out of this situation as much as you do. We don't know where we are, we can't even take a guess at how far we've been carried. The weather on this moon is so drokked up we could be a thousand kilometres away from where we started."

Vickers said, "You think we don't *know* that? Until the ice melts, we can't use the doors or windows. We don't have anything strong enough to cut through the roof; and for all we know, there's still a couple of metres of ice up there."

"So we go *down*," I said. "We go through the floor."

Eleven

WITHOUT PROPER TOOLS—the bus's toolbox was fixed to the outside—it took us almost two hours to undo the heavy bolts securing the access panel in the floor.

Once the bolts were removed, Guildford hacked through the thick silicon sealant around the panel with a screwdriver. "Okay. Everyone ready? Make sure your helmets are sealed, because once the air in here hits the methane, the moisture in the air will freeze and the methane will start to evaporate. You won't be able to breathe."

We gave him the all-clear, and he prised up the panel. The air clouded; the frost patterns on the windows briefly cleared before reforming into thick crystals.

Guildford pointed the one remaining flashlight down into the darkness. "Rico was right. It's liquid. Can't see much through it, but I think it's pretty deep."

"Can you swim through it?" asked Forbes.

"Not without a suit. I don't feel the cold and my skin is probably tough enough to survive it, but"— he tapped the voicebox at his throat—"This isn't waterproof. I'd drown."

"Then take one of the spare suits." I dropped down flat next to the hatch, and reached my gloved hand down into the thick liquid. "Triple insulated gloves and I can still feel it."

"You could put the other spare suit on over yours," suggested Pea. "That might help."

Montenegro shook her head. "He wouldn't be able to seal the second one. The methane would seep in, get trapped between the suits. That'd be worse."

Forbes handed me a roll of suit-repair tape. "This could work. I know it's only designed for small rips, but it'll help keep out the methane."

"No," I said. "It's hard enough to move in these suits as it is. I definitely wouldn't be able to swim wearing another one on top of it." There was a strong chance that I wouldn't make it more than a couple of metres, anyway, but there was no choice. It was either this or stay on the bus and suffocate.

I stood up again, watching as Forbes and Vickers helped Guildford into his suit.

Siebert passed me the large screwdriver, the only useful tool inside the bus. "You get us out of this and I'll talk to Copus. Get him to put in a word with the warden. I'll see what we can do to reduce your sentences."

"Sure," I said, but I didn't believe him. In the history of the prison, no one had ever had a sentence reduced. "Close it up after me. But if you hear me knocking, open it up *immediately*."

Siebert nodded. "Will do."

It was hard to be sure, through the helmet's visor and with his mutilated face, but it seemed to me that Guildford was grinning as he patted me on the shoulder. "I'll lead. I get into trouble, you head back, got that?"

Before I could answer, he was crouching down over the mist-obscured hatch and lowering himself into the liquid methane.

"Rico..." Pea said, "swim *fast*."

"Good thinking," I told him.

Register Forbes patted me on the shoulder. "Good luck, Rico. Whatever happens out there, you've earned my respect."

Yeah, that'll *do me a lot of good,* I said to myself as I followed Guildford down through the hatch. The instant my feet hit the liquid, they started to burn with the cold. I kept going; better to die quickly.

The methane was so cloudy with sand, dirt and swirls of oil and grease from the underside of the bus that I could barely see Guildford ahead of me.

We'd already agreed on the direction, the same way the bus was facing. The meagre sunlight seemed to be strongest that way, so we figured that the ice might have melted more on that side.

A hand swung down in front of my face, and I'm not ashamed to admit that I screamed.

The arm hung limply, drifting with the invisible currents, and it took me a moment to realise what it was. Another prisoner, suit mangled, faceplate crushed. Whoever he was, he had taken refuge under the bus when the storm hit, become entangled in the suspension mechanism.

How long? I wondered. *How long was he out there, only a metre away from the rest of us, and we didn't even know? He could have been screaming for help for* hours, *and we didn't hear him over the storm.*

Guildford hesitated too, but moved on, now upside-down as he kicked with his feet and used his hands to pull himself along the underside of the bus.

I followed, arms and legs already numb. The inside of my environment suit's visor had completely misted over, and I could only see Guildford as a thrashing shadow.

It seemed to take forever, though it was probably only seconds. Eventually the light ahead brightened as I reached the front of the bus and came out under the ice.

Guildford stopped in front of me and pointed up.

I looked. Maybe two metres overhead was a bright patch. Not an actual break in the ice, but a thin patch. Possibly thin enough to smash through.

Guildford kicked upward, braced his fists ahead of him and hit the underside of the ice. It didn't look as though he'd had an effect at all, but he wasn't giving up. He swam back down, pointed at me, locked his hands together in front of him, and again looked up.

I nodded and linked my hands, fingers locked, as though I was boosting him over a wall. He put one of his feet into my hands, and I hoisted him up while he kicked off.

Travelling a little faster this time, he again struck the ice with his fists.

Then we did it again. And again.

After the fifth attempt, Guildford shook his head and pointed off, suggesting that it might be better to try elsewhere.

But I wasn't ready to quit just yet, certainly wasn't willing to go searching for another thin patch, or for the edge of the ice. By now I could barely move, let alone boost him. The cold had seeped through into my bones, and every breath was like fire.

I held up my index finger—one more try—and this time I got him to boost me.

I saw the uneven, glassy ice approach, and at the last second I stabbed upward with the point of the screwdriver.

The impact rippled through my bones, threatened to tear my muscles free... But there was a crack in the ice. Without dropping back, I stabbed again, in the same spot, and the shock knocked the screwdriver from my grip. I grabbed for it, and missed.

I watched it drift down and I remember thinking, *This is* not *how I'm going to die! Not after everything!*

I was going to live out my twenty years on this glacial moon. I'd serve my time and go back to Earth, back to Mega-City One, and find my brother. Make him pay.

Because *he* did this to me. He had refused to see things from my point of view, to even consider the possibility that I'd been right. But that's how he's always been. Sure, he'll listen to advice and he'll pay attention to new ideas, but in the end Joe Dredd does whatever Joe Dredd wants.

And one day, I'd go back. I'd see him. Look the drokker in the eye and show him what he'd done.

Twenty years in this hell-hole for what? For having different ideas. For having the intelligence and the empathy to understand that the Law isn't everything. That without mercy, it's *nothing*.

Maybe it was because I was exhausted, and desperate. Maybe it was because I didn't like being trapped. Whatever it was, it fed my anger and my anger gave me strength.

I slammed my fist upwards, and it punched clear through the ice.

* * *

I KNEW THAT, inside my gloves, my knuckles were cracked, the skin raw and seeping, and I was grateful that I could feel nothing but the cold.

For a long time I didn't have the strength to pull myself up, so I clung to the edge of the fracture, trying to summon that anger again.

But it eluded me. All I could do was hold on, the faceplate of my environment suit barely above the misty surface of the liquid.

Through the soul-chilling numbness I felt Guildford's strong arms wrap themselves around my legs, and for a moment I imagined he was trying to pull me down, to drag me into the suffocating, freezing death.

Then he was lifting me from below, pushing me until I could get my elbows over the edge.

I hauled myself up, Guildford still pushing me, and collapsed onto the ice, face-down.

I allowed myself a couple of seconds to rest, then twisted around, reached into the hole, grabbed hold of Guildford's flailing hand, and pulled. It took the last of my strength to get him out, and I wouldn't have been able to do it had he not used the screwdriver—he'd seen it fall from my hand and caught it—as a piton.

It was only when he was out of the liquid and onto the ice that I understood how close we had come to failure. Twenty metres in front of us was the bus, trapped inside a hill of compacted hail. Guildford and I were in a shallow, inexplicable depression. Otherwise, the ice stretched for hundreds of metres in every direction.

The floe was drifting across a vast plain. There were mountains in the distance, but nothing recognisable. The only clue I had as to how far we'd come was the position of Saturn in the sky.

From where we were when the storm hit, Saturn should have been a few degrees above the horizon; here it was well up in the sky.

Guildford joined me, his helmet now removed, and we stood together looking at the planet. "What do you think, Rico? A couple of hundred kilometres?"

"At least," I said. "Probably a lot more."

"Then all that was for nothing. They're never going to find us before the oxygen in the suits runs out."

"*You'll* have to tell them what happened, then."

He barked a harsh, mechanical laugh, then slapped me on the shoulder. "We should get the others free. And then maybe there's a way we can break the bus loose. Probably won't work, but it'll keep us all occupied while death sneaks up on us."

We returned to the bus and circumnavigated it, looking for the easiest access point. As we walked, I told Guildford about the GPS fraud. He didn't seem surprised. He said, "They think we don't know, so we let them believe that. If they figure we know it's a con, they'll do it for real."

"How do *you* know?"

"I was a scientist, remember? And it doesn't take a genius—which I *am*, for whatever that's worth on this Grud-forsaken rock—to figure it out. You know how everyone keeps telling us that escape is impossible? Well, about four years ago three prisoners *did* escape. They weren't able to get off-planet, but they did manage to get out of the prison. Copus made a big show of bringing back the remains of their bodies, but it wasn't them. They'd dug up a few graves instead. For all we know the real escapees could still be out here somewhere." Guildford began to climb up onto the ice-sheathed front of the bus. "So they're free, but dead, of course, because there's nowhere on this rock to actually escape *to*."

I said, "Yeah, everyone keeps telling us *that*, too. But they're wrong."

Guildford looked back at me. "Meaning?"

"Meaning I'm pretty sure we're not alone on Titan."

Twelve

THE COMPACTED HAIL on top of the bus was a metre thick, and without proper tools the only way we could get through it was by hacking at it with the screwdriver and pulling at the chunks of ice with our hands. The constant freezing and thawing of the methane ice had solidified it into a single mass peppered with tiny pockets of air.

As we worked, we talked. "You look at the size of the prison's gardens," I told him, "then think of the portion sizes of our meals, and the number of prisoners. The gardens produce a lot more food than we consume. About three times as much."

"I guess the rest is used to create biofuel or ethanol to power the vehicles," said Guildford. He stamped the heel of his boot down onto the ice. "Like the bus. It's certainly not nuclear."

"That doesn't account for all of it," I said as I stabbed at what looked like a weak seam. "And every six days one particular truck heads out to pick up loose ore fragments. Or so they say. But from where? I've never been on that duty, nor has anyone I've asked. You've seen it—it's red and has a massive dent in the side of the cab. I've been keeping track... Sometimes it goes west, sometimes east, but that's a diversion. It always heads south." I dropped back, exhausted.

Guildford pulled the screwdriver from my hand, and took over. "How did you work *that* out?"

"Because *we're* sent out every direction but due south, and I've never seen the red truck out here, although I've seen every other one many times." I pushed myself to my feet, and turned in a slow circle. "And the red truck never comes back with a full load. In fact, it always comes back with pretty much the same amount of ore. Ore that *I've* never been assigned to unload. Have you?"

"Can't say that I have, no. So what are you saying? That there's another base somewhere on Titan and the prison is supplying it with food?"

"Yeah, I think so. It just carries the same ore out and back every time. And because they're keeping it a secret, I figure it's either a research station working on something big, or it's a military base."

Guildford stopped working, and turned to face me. "Military. Out *here*?"

"We know we're not alone in the galaxy. Have you ever heard of a society that *wasn't* paranoid about invaders? I'd put money on it, if I had any. There's a military base here. Probably one on every major moon in the system. And military bases have ships. And guns."

After some consideration, Guildford said, "If we knew exactly *where*..." Then he shook his head. "It'd be a lot better defended than the prison." He stepped back and handed me the screwdriver.

"I know," I said, as I crouched down and resumed working. We were above the roof of the bus, slowly working our way down through the ice toward the door. The plan was to clear away enough ice that Montenegro could get out, then she could take over for a while.

And we couldn't stop. Being a mod, Guildford had turned off his oxygen, but mine was already running low. When it was gone, I'd swap tanks with him, but even so, time was against us. The sooner we got Montenegro out, the sooner she could free the others.

We worked in silence for a while. Holding the screwdriver in both hands, I stabbed at the ice, over and over, while Guildford stood next to me, watching, ready to take over when the cold and constant jarring in my arms became too much.

"Suppose we *did* get to the military base," Guildford said, "And we managed to get a ship that we could somehow actually fly. What then? Where would we go? You've said it yourself many times—if we go back to Earth, we'll be shot down."

I told him, "We don't go to Earth. We go... elsewhere. There are races out there who'd pay a lot for our knowledge of Earth."

Before Guildford could reply, a head-sized portion of the ice collapsed under my hands.

We stared down into the small hole, and heard Siebert's voice call out, "We're through!"

It took another half-hour to free enough ice for Montenegro to squirm out.

Vickers came next. He threw a large cloth-wrapped bundle ahead of him, then reached for me and Guildford through the opening. "Don't try anything," he warned us. "Siebert's still armed. You don't want to lose your friends to a gun after all you've been through, right?"

We hauled him free, and he ordered us to back away. "Toward the front of the bus. Move." Still watching us, he called over his shoulder, "Mister Siebert? It's clear."

Vickers crouched down next to the opening and Siebert passed him up the gun.

Vickers held the gun on us as he tapped the bundle with his foot. "Spare oxygen tanks, the rest of the food and water. You'll be carrying it."

"Where are we going?" Guildford asked. "We don't know where we are, and—"

"No questions," Vickers said.

It was a few minutes before Register Forbes emerged, clambering awkwardly out of the hole, almost slipping back a couple of times. He hoisted his stomach over the edge, then turned to help Siebert out.

Siebert was also carrying a large bundle, and I could see now that they'd been fashioned from the thick rubberised cloth that covered the seats inside the bus.

Vickers helped the other guards out, Guildford, Montenegro and I watching, as Siebert and Forbes peered around at our surroundings.

"I don't know this place," Forbes said. "We could be anywhere. What do we do?"

Siebert examined his gun. "We have one high-ex shell. We can use that as a flare if we see anything. Right now, we head west." Then he looked directly at me. "You were right about the military base."

"You heard that," I said.

"We heard *everything,*" Siebert said. He kicked at the bundle at his feet, and it slid over the ice toward me. "Pick it up. You three walk ahead of us, not more than ten metres, not closer than five. We stop only when *I* say we stop. Understood?"

"What about the others?" asked Montenegro. "We can't just leave them here!"

Even before I picked up the bundle, I knew what had happened. It was heavier than it should have been, and that was because it contained more oxygen tanks. Not just the tanks from the spare suits. "There *are* no others," I told her. "They're dead."

Thirteen

NAVIGATING ON TITAN isn't as tough as it would be on Earth, where the sun is only a useful pointer if you know the time of day. Titan's day is the same length as its orbit, so Saturn never moves in the sky. If we'd been on the other side of Titan, it's almost certain that none of us would have made it.

The ice-floe continued to melt as we walked, in pockets that evaporated into thick, tall columns of mist that twisted and writhed like giant agonised snakes. In some places, the mist remained at ground level, hiding the deep, jagged-edged pits from which it had evaporated.

Forbes and the guards walked behind us, mostly in silence but occasionally talking or even joking.

I couldn't take my mind off the prisoners inside the bus. I didn't know most of them—Pea was the only one I'd have considered a friend—but that wasn't the point.

Siebert had ordered them killed just to give himself a better chance of survival. And I had no doubt that if they hadn't needed me, Montenegro and Guildford to carry their supplies, we too would have been left behind.

After a few hours, the wind picked up a little, coming at us from behind, blowing away the mist and allowing us sporadic glimpses of the pockmarked landscape ahead. The wind was loud enough that the guards could no longer hear us talk.

"They won't admit what they've done," I told Guildford and Montenegro. "They'll kill us before we reach the military base."

Montenegro said, "So we have to remain useful to them as long as possible. And that means not using up the supplies too quickly."

A few minutes later we lost one of the guards. Frazier, a quiet man who'd always looked to me like he was continually running a mental countdown of the days he had left until retirement, walked across a patch of ordinary-looking ice and it cracked under his feet.

The rest of us barely had time to register the sound of the crack before he was gone: fallen through, dragged under by the liquid methane's strong current, and swept away. It took a second, maybe less.

Frazier had been carrying one of the makeshift sacks of supplies.

We carried on—there was nothing else we *could* do—with increased caution, and growing concern from Guildford. He sidled closer to me. "Most of my food-paste was in Frazier's pack."

"The rest of us will share," I told him.

He tapped his grey, surgically-sealed mouth. "I can only eat the paste, remember?"

There was a solution to that, of course, as we discovered on our next food-break. The environment suits featured a small airlock on the underside of the helmet, so that non-mod prisoners working outside could eat by breaking up the food and inserting it one mouthful at a time. The food was compacted lumps of dried fruit and vegetables. We'd break off a chunk, put it into the food-airlock where it'd be warmed up.

That wouldn't work for Guildford—he couldn't chew. So I had to do the work for him, and that wasn't pleasant for any of us. I took his meagre portion of food and chewed it up, spat it back out into his hand so he could quickly force it into the voicebox-hole in his throat before it froze.

Vickers and one of the other guards—I never learned his name—thought this was tremendously amusing.

We reached the edge of the ice-floe shortly after that, and by luck it had butted up against a gentle hillside. If we'd had to wade through the lake of liquid methane I doubt any of us would have survived.

We trudged on through the Bronze, sleeping a few hours at a time whenever Siebert grew too tired to carry on. We left in our wake a widely-spaced trail of discarded oxygen tanks and food packaging, until Montenegro, Guildford and I could no longer fake how light the makeshift bags had grown.

Siebert ordered a stop. "Food and water are getting low, and night's coming in. We don't need all three of you to carry the gear. You can decide amongst yourselves which of you won't be coming any further."

Montenegro said, "Siebert, if you show up at the military base with Forbes as the only surviving prisoner, they'll figure out what happened. No matter what we've done, you have a duty of care to your prisoners, and—"

Siebert shot her in the face.

I HAD ALREADY decided to kill Siebert, so the suddenness and brutality of his action made little difference to how I felt. But it did crystallise the timetable. Siebert and the others, Forbes included, had to die before they killed me. Or Guildford; I'd never make it to the military base alone.

But I needed Siebert alive to *find* the place. That was the only reason I hadn't already smashed open his helmet and watched him suffocate.

"Rico, get her tank and supplies," Siebert ordered. "Then we pick up the pace. It won't be much longer now. We get within a hundred kilometres of the base, they'll detect us and send someone out to investigate."

Guildford and I took a last look at Montenegro as we removed the oxygen tank from her suit. While we crouched over her he quietly asked me, "You still got Siebert's key?"

"Yeah. Can't see what good it'll do us, though. We're not chained."

"It's got a power-source. First chance you get, give it to me."

We marched on, always heading west. Though Guildford was bigger and stronger than me, and had been adapted for the climate, he wasn't holding up too well. Maybe it was because I'd been trained as a Judge. Or maybe it was because, despite everything, Donny Guildford of Brit-Cit wasn't used to seeing someone he knew gunned down in cold blood.

He spoke about that as we walked. He'd rarely mentioned anything about his past before, and I knew then that he was certain that he was going to die. This was his confession. Perhaps telling it to a Judge made things easier, I don't know. But I listened, because he was my friend.

"I did it," he told me. "There. Never admitted it before, not even when the prosecution showed absolute proof. I did it. I killed them. Deliberately, too. I intended to kill them, and I succeeded."

"So who were they?" I asked.

"Colleagues. One in particular. We were working on a way to create liquid glass." He turned to me and smiled, as best as his sewn-up mouth allowed. "Pointless, I know. There's not a lot of practical applications, but we weren't exactly in a cutting-edge industry. Everyone thinks that research scientists spend their days trying to come up with a smarter rat-trap or a cure for something horrible, but most of us are in the private sector working on stuff intended to save a private company tiny sums of money. Liquid glass was probably going to be a novelty item. It'd be liquid at room temperature." Guildford shrugged. "Like I said, pointless."

Behind us, Vickers called out, "Shut up!"

I shouted back, "Why?"

He didn't have a real answer for that. "Because I said so!"

Guildford resumed talking anyway. "So, there was this guy in the company, one of those people who just really wind you up the wrong way. They never actually do anything bad, nothing you can point your finger at and say, '*That's* why he's a complete spugwit!' but still, you can't get along with them. You know the type?"

I said that I did. I was, of course, thinking of Little Joe.

"Herman, his name was. He joined the company after I did, and everyone liked him immediately. *I* did too, for a while. But Herman just kept pushing my buttons, over and over. Wouldn't stop no matter what I said or did. It was stupid stuff, mostly. Like, we'd go together to the canteen for lunch, and he always—*always*—ended up ahead of me in the line. Somehow, we'd be walking along the corridor and no matter what I did, it was always me holding the door open for him, so that he'd go through first and go straight to the end of the line." Guildford shrugged. "Like I said, stupid stuff.

But imagine that happening every single day for eight drokkin' *years*."

I was about to make a comment, but he wasn't done yet.

"Herman always found a way to get under my skin. Subtle things, but the sort that build up. Leaving stuff on my desk. Taking my pen and chewing the end of it. And he'd go out with the others after work and not invite me, but the next day he'd tell me what a great night it was, and that I should have been there."

There was more like this, a *lot* more, and it was all I could do to rein in my Judge training and resist punching his arm and telling him to grow a pair. What it all boiled down to was that this guy Herman had supplanted him in the company's social hierarchy, and so Guildford poisoned him with thallium. "It was simple, in the end," Guildford said. "I dipped my pen in thallium dust and left it on my desk. I mean, I'd told Herman a hundred times not to chew my pens, but, true to form, he did it anyway."

"How did you get caught?" I asked.

"Well, Herman was only the first. I had problems with another colleague, in a different department. We'd talk about work and he'd take my ideas and present them to his boss like he'd thought of them. So he had to go. So did his boss; that drokker *knew* they were my ideas and he didn't care. And there was a neighbour, too. And a few others."

"How many in total? Someone told me it was at least ten, is that right?"

"Seventeen. They caught me because some hot-shot young Judge took over the investigation and just wouldn't let it go."

After a long pause, I said, "*I'd* have executed you on the spot."

"I know. But that was Brit-Cit, not Mega-City One. You have your Laws, we have ours."

I glanced back at our captors. "And here, they have their *own* laws. It all seems so... arbitrary."

An hour later, Siebert called for another rest-break. Guildford and I strolled back to the others, but kept our distance.

Vickers dropped to the ground and said, "We must have walked a thousand kilometres by now."

"A couple of hundred, at most," I told him. To Siebert, who was gulping water from his bottle, I said, "Slow down. We don't know how long we'll be out here."

Siebert glared at me. "You don't tell me what to do, Rico. *Never* tell me what to do." He looked around to make sure the others were listening, then said, "Rico Dredd was a Judge, can you believe that? A *Judge*. Supposed to be the best of the best. Turned out he was nothing but a thug. A perp. Best-trained perp in the world, maybe, but still a bottom-feeder. Still nothing more than a piece of murdering scum." Siebert lowered himself down to the ground next to Vickers. "You think your old man would be proud of you, Rico? I doubt it. He'd have put you away himself. Like your brother did."

Standing close to them, Register Forbes said, quietly, "Siebert, it's time."

"Yeah, I know." Siebert looked from me to Guildford and back. "One of you has come to the end of his journey. And it's *you*, Rico. We still need one of you to carry the stuff, and Guildford doesn't need an oxygen tank." He smiled. "Told you I'd reduce your sentence if you got us out of the bus, didn't I?"

"I understand," I said. "Believe me, if I was in your position I'd do the same. Give me a few minutes to make my peace with Grud?"

"Never took you for a believer, Rico. But go ahead. Say whatever prayers you think might help you. But try not to breathe too much—no sense in wasting that precious oxygen."

"Of course." I dropped to my knees, facing away from them. I took a few deep breaths, then disconnected the tank from my suit. Hidden in the palm of my other hand I had Siebert's electronic key.

Guildford had explained how it worked. It was about the size of a thumb, and the only reason it needed to be that big was because it contained a thumb-scanner. When Siebert wanted to unlock a chain, he put his thumb on the scanner, the key's internal circuits recognised it, and for the next one hundred seconds it would disable the appropriate lock. But I didn't care about the scanner, or the circuitry. I was interested in the tiny lithium battery inside the lock.

It had been tricky work, with the insulated gloves, but I'd managed to disconnect the battery from the rest of the key, exposing the hair-thin wires.

Guildford said, "I don't want to see this. Been nice knowing you, Rico." He walked away.

There was no time to experiment, to check that what I was planning was even possible. When you're a Judge, you're trained to work with whatever you have to hand.

I had a half-full oxygen tank, a methane-rich atmosphere and a device capable of making a spark.

Behind me, Siebert got to his feet and said, "You've had long enough. You'll be seeing Grud in person in a few seconds anyway."

"Okay," I said. I stood up, and turned to face him. I had the oxygen tank, with the key taped to it, in my left hand.

All four remaining guards, and Forbes, were clustered nicely. The explosion, if it worked, would certainly take them all out. But it would take me out too. Guildford and I had talked about that, and agreed that it was worth it if only one of us was going to make it.

I honestly believed that was *it* for me, that I was going to die right there and then. It might have looked like a noble sacrifice to save my friend, but the truth is that I just wanted those drokkers to suffer.

Forbes said to me, "Rico, no hard feelings. You understand that this is how it's got to be?"

"You'll be next, Forbes. They need Guildford alive more than they need you."

"I doubt it," he said, smiling. "If I die under suspicious circumstances, certain information about certain guards will become public. Right, Siebert?"

"That's right," the guard said, nodding.

I said to Forbes, "I know this is coming a bit late, but you wanted me to shake your hand, first time we met. I refused." I extended my right hand to him. "Well done. I'm man enough to admit that you beat me. But don't die *here,* Forbes, got that? Don't let them win. At least *one* of us has to get out of this alive."

Forbes shook my hand, a smug little grin on his face. "Sure, Rico."

I stepped closer to him, turning the handshake half-way into a friendly embrace. With my left hand around his back.

Vickers said, "Wait, what's that he's got—?"

He never finished that sentence, because I pressed my thumb into the inside of the key. The battery's exposed wires sparked, and ignited the pure oxygen invisibly spraying from the tank's half-open valve.

I let the tank go and whipped my hand back just as the tank exploded. Forbes slammed against me, shielding me from the blast as shards of the tank tore through the guards.

One shard, quite a large one, passed straight through Vickers's chest. He was the first of them to die. The others merely had their suits ripped open. There was plenty of repair tape, of course, but that was with the bundles of supplies that Guildford and I had been carrying.

The guards desperately tried to cover the rips in their environment suits. Siebert ran for the supplies, and Guildford tackled him from behind, brought him crashing face-first onto the frozen ground.

My own suit had been torn, too. Not as much as Forbes's had, but enough that I was losing air, and fast.

I rolled Forbes's mangled body off me, then scrambled to my feet.

I ran past Guildford, who was sitting on top of Siebert's prone body and methodically slamming the screaming man's face into a sharp-pointed rock, and skidded to a stop next to the supplies.

Obviously I survived. I'm still around to tell the tale.

Siebert didn't. Guildford cracked the face-plate on his suit, and—ignoring my suggestion that we sit and watch him die—continued to slam his face against the rock. Over and over, until I swear I could see the rock making dents in the back of Siebert's helmet.

GUILDFORD DIED SIX days later.

We'd carried on walking, always going west, because the only other option was to lay down and die.

We dragged the supplies behind us, and as the days progressed that became both easier and harder. Easier because there was less and less to drag, harder because we'd run out of food and fresh water.

The environment suits are capable of recycling the body's waste water—sweat and urine—but that only works for so long before the filters become clogged.

Night had fallen on Titan, but there was enough light from Saturn that we could mostly see where we were going. Mostly, but not perfectly. Guildford stepped on a loose rock, tripped, and his left ankle snapped.

He couldn't walk, and I didn't have the strength to carry him.

I had Siebert's gun—there was no way I was going to leave *that* behind—and Guildford begged me to put him out of his misery.

"Do it, Rico! Make it fast. I've always known I wasn't getting off this rock. Better to end it now, because even if we get back, I don't think I can last another week in the prison." He looked up at me, through plastic-coated eyes that, if they'd been capable, would have filled with tears. "I *deserve* to die, Rico. I murdered all those people because I cared more about my feelings than I did about their lives. So do it. Shoot me."

I looked down at him, and did my best to give him a brave smile. "Good-bye, Donny."

The echo of the shot seemed to last a lot longer than it should have. Maybe that was the strange atmosphere on Titan, or maybe it was just my imagination.

Fourteen

I DON'T KNOW who found me. I asked, but they wouldn't tell me. The last thing I remember, when I couldn't go on any further, was using the high-explosive shell in Siebert's gun to blast a large chunk out of the side of a hill, in the hope that someone would see the explosion and come looking.

I guess it worked. Hell, for all I know, the military base could have been on the other side of that hill.

I woke up in the prison infirmary, surrounded by too-familiar sounds and smells. And I was glad to be back; the only alternative was a slow, suffocating death. I'd no idea how long I'd been unconscious, or how I got there. All I knew was that I was alive and, for the first time in an eternity, I wasn't hungry or thirsty.

I couldn't see too well—everything seemed out-of-focus—and I couldn't move, could barely even turn my head, and it took me a few moments to understand that I'd been strapped to the bed.

On my left side a hazy face came into view, close enough for me to recognise it as sub-warden Copus. I was genuinely pleased to see the man.

"Don't try to talk, Rico. You probably can't, anyway. You've been through quite an ordeal. Twenty-five went out, only one came back." Copus moved closer in an odd jarring motion, and I realised he was sitting on a chair and had shuffled forward. "We backtracked your path... Found a few of the others. Took us some time to identify Siebert." He paused for a long time, then said, "There were a couple of hidden cameras on the bus. Siebert and his friends weren't aware of them. So we know a lot of what happened. The bus got trapped in that hailstorm, is that right?"

I nodded.

"You and Guildford managed to get out. You freed the others. Then Siebert decided you should all head for... a place he'd heard about. Correct?"

Again, I nodded.

"That place doesn't exist, Rico. You know that, don't you? It *can't* exist. Siebert was delusional, or maybe he was lying in order to keep morale up, to give you the motivation you all needed to survive. I *know* that's what it was, because there's nothing on this moon but us. Only us." Copus leaned back a little, and seemed to be lost in thought for a moment. "I was never able to prove that Siebert was dirty, but the hidden cameras caught him and Frazier strangling the other prisoners to increase their own chances of survival."

Then, more to himself than to me, he added, "We're gonna have to make some changes around here. *Big* changes. It was a mistake to have Register Forbes serve his sentence in the same place he committed his crimes."

He looked at me again. "But *you*, Rico... Fact is you probably should have been left out there. Your return has been giving the other inmates the idea that it's possible to survive out on the surface. That's not what we want. Not what we want at all. So the warden and I made a decision. You understand that this was the only way, right?"

This time, I shook my head. I had no idea what he was talking about.

Copus's head moved out of view and I felt him working at the straps holding my left arm in place. "Raise your arm," he told me.

I did so, and though I couldn't see it too clearly, it seemed that it was thinner than before. That was reasonable, after what I'd gone through. But I didn't expect my skin to be grey.

When Copus said, "We had to make some modifications," I understood why my vision was blurred.

* * *

A WEEK LATER I was released from the infirmary and returned to the general population. No one would look me in the eye, and I don't blame them. I could barely look *myself* in the eye.

They turned me into a monster. Not because they had to, but because they *wanted* to. They were in charge, and they wanted the other prisoners to understand that.

Guildford had been right about the memory-altering drugs they'd administered before the operation: I have absolutely no recollection of it. And he was also right about the pain afterwards. Breathing and blinking were agony for the first few days. Took me a long time to get used to the new sensations.

But it's nice not to feel the cold any more.

Before I left the infirmary, Copus told me, "When your time here is done, we'll reverse the process. You'll be left with some scarring, but..." He shrugged. "Until then, you *play ball,* Rico. There is no military establishment on Titan."

I said, "I understand. I genuinely do. I was a Judge, remember? A damn good one. I understand the need for secrets. And who would I *tell,* Copus? All of my friends are dead." I looked at him steadily for a few seconds. "They all died in the storm. It was only by luck that I managed to survive."

What they did to me was horrific, but—from their point of view—it was necessary.

There's an upside, I can't deny that. Copus arranged with the warden that my sentence should be reduced. Officially, that was in light of what Guildford and I did to free the others. Unofficially, it was a bribe to encourage me to forget about the military base that they denied existed. Plus, let's be honest here, I'd been a model prisoner. Never started any trouble, never tried to escape. Being turned into a freak is fair price for getting out a year early.

And mods work ten-hour shifts instead of the usual twelve. I use those extra two hours to read, or work out, or play chess with anyone brave enough to take me on.

I have to keep myself sharp, you see, because I *will* get out. One day, I'll return to Mega-City One and then... And then Little Joe and I will settle things. We'll talk, he and I. And I know I'll be able to prove to him that I was right all along.

Justice must be tempered with mercy. It must be flexible, and that goes both ways. Sure, what Copus and the warden did to me is inhumane, but it was necessary for the greater good. They had no reason to trust me not to say anything, and they didn't want to just execute me, so they came up with a compromise. It's not a perfect solution for any of us, but it *works*.

It's just like it was back in the Meg. What happened with Virgil Livingstone, well, that was an accident. He shouldn't have died. No, scratch that. I shouldn't have killed him. But I was making a point about the Law, and it's a point in which I still believe: If the Law is too rigid, the citizens will eventually rise against it. But if it bends, even just a little, then the citizens will come to understand and respect that.

The Judges present themselves as untouchable, as incorruptible, and the people don't like that. They don't like being made to feel inferior. The way *I* ran things, that wasn't the case. Sure, it was clear to everyone that I was on the top of the heap, but they knew that they could come to me. They knew that I could change the things that needed to be changed. The other Judges said, "This is the Law, and it is immutable. Put up or shut up." Okay, so it's not actually immutable, since the Judges change the Law as they see fit, but that's part of the problem. They change it to suit themselves, not to suit the citizens.

Is it any wonder that they're despised?

In my year on the streets of Mega-City One, I worked hard to be seen as one of the people, and I know that they respected that. They respect a Judge who, if he catches them littering, will slap them across the back of the head and tell them not to do it again. They don't respect a Judge who'll imprison them for it.

So I'll get out of here when my time is done.

I'll go back to Earth. To Mega-City One.

And I'll find my brother.

And then we'll see who was right.

Then we'll see.

About the Author

Irish Author **Michael Carroll** is a former chairperson of the Irish Science Fiction Association and has previously worked as a postman and a computer programmer/systems analyst. A reader of *2000 AD* right from the very beginning, Michael is the creator of the acclaimed *Quantum Prophecy/Super Human* series of superhero novels for the Young Adult market.

His current comic work includes *Judge Dredd* for *2000 AD* and *Judge Dredd Megazine* (Rebellion), and *Jennifer Blood* (Dynamite Entertainment).

www.michaelowencarroll.com

Coming soon:

RICO DREDD: THE TITAN YEARS

THE PROCESS OF ELIMINATION

Read a teaser now...

Chapter One

It's said that even the toughest prisoner is no match for Titan. *Everyone* breaks, they say.

The cold, the storms, the darkness, the endless labour, the sporadic nocturnal screaming sessions, the ever-present danger from the guards and the other prisoners, the days that last three hundred and eighty-two hours, the constant risk of suffocation in Titan's toxic air, the food so utterly bland that sometimes you'd happily murder everyone on the whole drokkin' moon just for the chance to lick the pot a potato had been boiled in.

Most prisoners broke, eventually; a few didn't. I didn't. Never broke down, never once allowed myself to roll over and expose that emotional underbelly. Displaying a weakness like that in such a hostile environment is the equivalent of handing the other guy a gun and showing him where on your chest you wanted him to aim.

Cadmus Robert Holland—male, Caucasian, fifty-something—finally crumbled, more than a year into his sentence. We'd long since exhausted the pool on him and just taken it as solid that he wasn't going to crack.

We all knew *why* Holland was there, of course, known that from the start. He'd murdered his brother. Bludgeoned him to death with his fists in a frenzy of pure rage. For someone not trained in hand-to-hand combat, that's a pretty impressive feat. Sure, anyone can knock someone over so they hit their head and that kills them, but to actually cave in a human skull using only your knuckles? That takes a special kind of fury.

Otherwise, the only remarkable thing about Cadmus Holland was that he was one of the final batch of Mega-City One citizens sentenced to Titan. Other cities kept sending civilians for the next few years, but someone in the Big Meg had decided that the mining colony on Titan was too harsh a punishment for cits, and fit only for wayward Judges.

It was late November, 2084. A bunch of us had been assigned to cable-duty on J-shaft. Assignments were usually fixed, and most of the time I was outside the prison compound, but sometimes a dig would be picked clean and we'd have to wait until another one was found; or sometimes, the weather was just too bad. That was when they put us on J. It wasn't the worst duty—that would be waste management, and believe me, you do *not* want to know the details—but it was hard work, especially pulley duty.

The shaft was inside the prison compound, and was the primary reason the prison had been built just there. A rich, almost vertical seam of iridium ore that even after all these years still hadn't been exhausted. The yield was about a kilogramme of iridium for every two tonnes we dug out. That might not sound like much, but it gave the average astrogeologist palpitations.

The shaft was a narrow cone, fifty metres across at the surface and three hundred metres deep, with a few small side-tunnels that snaked away, following smaller deposits. It was covered by a sturdy, three-storey-high framework, housing thirty or so mechanical pulley blocks.

That day, former Sov Judge Zera Kurya and I joined eighteen other prisoners hauling on the pulley cables, two prisoners to a cable. We nodded the usual greetings to the teams on either side of us—Cadmus Holland and Artherus Schiller were on our right—and then untied our cables and started to pull.

Arm over arm, steadily hoisting up huge steel buckets of ore. When they reached the pulley block, we switched to a second cable that pulled the bucket forward until it was clear of the pit, then tipped it into the back of a waiting truck.

The trucks took the ore to the smelter, which refined the metal, depositing bars of iridium in neat stacks. Back on Earth, any one of those bars could set someone up for life. Here on Titan, they were just piled up, waiting for the next ship to collect them.

It took an average of four hundred arm-pulls to get a bucket up from the lowest level of the pit. I know: I'd counted. It was exhausting, tedious, back-breaking work and everyone hated it. Most jobs in the prison you'd find someone who didn't mind it, but not this.

New fish always think that they'll be okay with it, and for the first few hours it's not so bad. The buckets weigh about half a tonne fully laden; but with two people lifting, that's only two-hundred and fifty kilogrammes each. And the pulley block has a ten-to-one ratio—for every metre you pull, the bucket is raised ten centimetres—so you're really only lifting twenty-five kilograms. In Titan's low gravity, that's hardly any work at all.

Until you have to do it over and over, a twelve-hour shift, in your bulky, uncomfortable environment suit, on your feet the whole time. You get three twenty-minute breaks per shift, and no talking if certain guards are supervising.

I had it a little easier because mods only do ten-hour shifts when we're working outside: after that, we have to purge our sinus filters, and no one wants to see that.

Six hours into the shift our supervising guard, Delaney, called second break. Delaney was a barrel-chested man with rosy cheeks and white bushy eyebrows. Donny Guildford had once whispered to me that he looked like Santa Claus had gone into witness protection, and it'd stuck with me ever since. We liked him; he was one of those guards who wasn't paranoid enough to equate casual conversation with sedition.

As we all gratefully tied off our cables and sat down on the frozen ground, Cadmus Holland said, "I'm done."

Artherus Schiller asked, "You've done what?"

Inside his helmet, Holland slowly shook his head. "I can't go on. This drokkin' place... The air is poison, nothing grows in the frozen dirt, the storms wind can tear you apart. And for what? For *this*." He picked up a small chunk of rock and bounced it in the palm of his hand. "Iridium." He pointed straight up. "There are whole *asteroids* made of the stuff up there. Much closer to home than we are." To Kurya, he said, "I heard your people are talking about setting up a mass-driver in the asteroid belt. Shoot the damn things at Earth, let them burn up in the atmosphere, save the cost of smelting them to get the ore out. That's the way it should be done."

"Probably wasn't their idea," Schiller said. "The Sovs don't invent. They just take other people's ideas. You know? Communism. Even the ideas belong to the state. No offence, Kurya."

"Die in pain," she responded calmly.

I said, "Schiller, shut that down right now. And you can drop the 'I can't take it any more' attitude too, Holland. You can and you will. Your first week, you thought you weren't going to survive, am I right?"

He nodded. "Yeah, but—"

"You were wrong then. Never thought you'd make it through your first month either, or your first year. Same as the rest of us. But you were wrong then too. You *did* make it. Now you think you can't make it to the end of your sentence. What makes you right about that when you were wrong before?"

Schiller gave a half-laugh, half-snort. "Dredd's right. You'll get back to Earth. Start your life over."

Then Holland said, "Without my brother."

"Yeah, well, *you're* the one who caved in his skull. You crack an egg, you can't go complaining that the yolk is leaking out, right?"

Normally, Holland would have either completely ignored that, or responded with a brisk head-butt. This time, he just nodded.

Schiller flashed me a look that said, *That's interesting...* Then he asked, "Why'd you do it, Holland? You spent eighteen years taking care of your brother, and then one day you just snapped."

Holland sighed long and deep, and the strength and life just seemed to slip out of him like a punctured airbed.

I knew from previous conversations that Holland had grown up believing in Mega-City One, in the Justice Department. He'd lost friends and family in the war—on both sides—but had never lost his faith in humanity. In the end, no matter what the odds, the good in people will triumph.

That's what he believed. That was at the core of Cadmus Robert Holland's being: the notion that people are inherently good. There are some who stray from time to time, but there is always a nucleus of goodness deep inside even the most hardened, most bloodthirsty criminal.

I guess he was right about that. Back in the Meg I got to know a lot of people who have one foot firmly in the gutter. The department classifies them as criminals, but ignores the good that they do. A woman can spend her entire life and all her pay making clothes for the homeless, but she shoplifts one can of lettuce-freshener and she's labelled a thief.

I've already mentioned my friend Evan Quasarano. Grew up in the ghetto, joined a gang, became a small-time crook. Why'd he do that? Because he knew nothing else. His mother struggled to keep the family fed and clothed, his father was long gone and his grandfathers constantly bickered. They'd been on different sides during the war and every family get-together was destined to go down the 'What the *drokk* did you just say?' route. More than once I'd had to pry the two old guys apart, stop them from killing each other over the dinner table.

Evan was a thief, a thug, a lowlife numbers-runner and occasional bodyguard. All before his eighteenth birthday. Did that make him a bad person? No, just misguided. I'd spent a lot of time with him, listening to his barely-formed opinions and regurgitations of other people's ideas, and I could tell that Evan was just ignorant, and maybe a bit dumb. But I once saw him give half a bag of crawbies to a kid who'd had his own stash stolen before he could sell it, all because he knew that kid's mother would have beaten him if he'd come home empty-handed. You can't tell me *that's* something a bad person would do.

People are a little selfish, maybe, but when they take the time to step outside their own lives and see things from other perspectives, they generally do realise that we're all in this together. I'm not saying that it's altruism, doing good for no reward or recognition, but that's not the point. Every good thing we do helps make the world a better place—and who doesn't want to live in a better world?

That had always been Cadmus Holland's stance. Broderick—his younger brother—had apparently been a nice guy, doing pretty well at school, had some good friends. He'd been well-adjusted and well-liked by most people.

Holland said, "Something happened to him the day after a bunch of us went to the Festival of Wheels."

Schiller said, "I remember that. We couldn't go—Papa said it was too expensive to get to Mega-City One."

Holland nodded slowly for a moment, then calmly said, "You've been begging me forever to tell you, so shut the drokk up and listen."

Schiller grinned. He was never the sort to take offence easily.

"Broderick was thirteen years old," Holland said. "We'd had a good time at the festival but the next morning he didn't respond when I woke him up for school. I mean, he got up, but he didn't say anything. Went off to school still not talking to me. I figured he was angry with me for something, but you know kids—you can't read their minds. That night I got a call from his school. Broderick hadn't spoken to anyone all day, not even when his teachers asked him directly.

"So I went into his room and said, 'The hell's the matter with you?' Nothing. 'You're not talking to me?' Still nothing. I figured it would blow over in a few days, but I was wrong. I could see it in his eyes sometimes that he *wanted* to speak, but he just couldn't. I gave him a pencil and a pad, but he just threw them aside. Same with the datapad. After the second week I brought him to the doctor. Those first brain-scans alone cost me a month's salary, but they didn't show up anything wrong. No damage, no lesions, no parasites. Broderick had just lost the ability, or the will, to speak.

"We did have some medical insurance, but the drokkers refused to pay up without an official diagnosis, so I had to pay for everything. Sold the car. Sold the house to cover a four-week stint in the Tremaine Clinic, but still they couldn't find anything wrong. Had to move into a crappy one-bedroom stomm-hole on the west side after that. And then..." Holland looked up. "*That* day. Broderick was thirty. We'd been living with his condition for seventeen *years*. We were out, scouring the market down under the flyovers... I thought that maybe I could get him a job somewhere that it didn't matter that he couldn't speak. At that stage we were so broke I was dealing zizz to juves. So we saw this market stand where an old guy was selling dead-shirts. He—"

Kurya interrupted. "Dead-shirts?"

I answered for him. "Clothing taken from bodies at Resyk. Used to be that the Resyk centres just incinerated the stiffs' shoes and clothing, but then they started using it as landfill. Some people steal the clothes from the landfills and sell them. It was actually quite the fashion for a while. I remember—" I caught the look in Holland's eye. "Sorry. Go on."

Holland said, "I asked the old guy if he needed help getting the stuff, and he said, 'Yeah, maybe. Not easy work, though. You strong?' I said, 'I am, but it's not me looking for the job. It's my brother Broderick here.'

"And then Broderick said, 'It's about drokkin' time!'"

Kurya said, "So he had *not* lost the ability to speak?"

"No. No, he hadn't. I asked him what the hell was going on, and he told me that seventeen years earlier, the night before that first morning, just before he went to bed... We'd been joking about someone we knew. He didn't even remember *who* it was, but that's not important. What *is* important is that we both said, 'Yeah, that guy's *insane!*' at the same time. And... and then *I* said, 'Jinx.'"

We all stared at Holland.

Schiller muttered, "Stomm..."

I said, "No way. No *way* he kept that up for seventeen years!"

Holland said, "He did. Stubborn little *drokker*. That was the rule, see. Two of you say the same thing at the same time, then if one of you says 'jinx' before either of you say anything else, then the other one can't speak until the first one says their name."

Schiller asked, "In all that time you never said his name? Not even when you were speaking to a doctor about him?"

"Sure I did, but apparently not when he was around to hear me use it. He said I'd just referred to him as 'my brother.'" Holland stared down at his hands. "I'd put my entire life aside and spent every credit we had trying to find out what was wrong with him and he could have put a stop to it at any time with a note on a scrap of paper. So I hit him. And I couldn't stop. He was long dead by the time the Judges came, and even then they had to shoot me to get me away from him."

No one could think of anything to say after that.

WWW.ABADDONBOOKS.COM

Follow us on Twitter! www.twitter.com/rebellionpub

FIND US ONLINE!

www.rebellionpublishing.com

/rebellionpub /rebellionpublishing /rebellionpub

SIGN UP TO OUR NEWSLETTER!

rebellionpublishing.com/sign-up

YOUR REVIEWS MATTER!

Enjoy this book? Got something to say?

Leave a review on Amazon, GoodReads or with your favourite bookseller and let the world know!

37680130R00072

Printed in Great Britain
by Amazon